RUNNING DRY

M.CHRISTIAN

ISBN: 979-8-9918668-2-8

Cover: KaNaXa Design
Interior Design: Terry Roy of Teryvisions

CONTENTS

CONTENTS, *continued*

For Jill

INTRODUCTION

Everything—and everyone—has to start somewhere, like how this book and I, as a novelist, began with a short story.

Three-something years after selling "Intercore" to *Future Sex Magazine*, which was then chosen by Susie Bright for *Best American Erotica 1994*, I, and what Patrick Califia dubbed my fellow "Glamorous Nerd Pornographers," were submitting as many stories to as many anthologies as we could.

My tightknit merry little band of festive smuteteers did a lot of share-and-sharing alike back then, as in "when I edit an anthology, I invite you" and "when you edit an anthology, you invite me"—which also explains why the same names appear over and over again in 1990s erotica. Though nepotism only got you so far, which I like to believe kept us on our literary toesies.

So I was honored when my pal, Thomas S. Roche, and his co-editor, Michael Rowe, asked me to send them something for their anthology, *Sons of Darkness: Tales of Men, Blood and Immortality*.

Yes, I was honored, but I was also gosh-darned terrified. Thomas and Michael wanting an erotic story wasn't it, as by then, I had fifty-plus of them already under my belt. Neither did I quiver in my combat boots at the prospect of writing LGBTQIA2S+ fiction, as a sizable hunk of those stories were precisely that.

Vampires…it was vampires, though not in a nightmare-fueled paralysis, wracked with goose-pimpling, dreadful sort of way. If I was, I could've at least channeled my creature-of-the-night anxieties into my submission.

Nope, it was—and still is—and no insult to Thomas, Michael, and all you other fang-fans out there, I was very, very, *very* tired of them. From *Interview with a Vampire* to *Buffy* to *The Vampire Chronicles*, the 90s were a decade of bloodsuckers. It was a genre that refused to die (like zombies in the 2020s).

In the end, I faced my fears (and boredom), and "Wet" didn't just make it into *Sons of Darkness*, but I remain quite fond of it—especially as it inspired my first novel, *Running Dry.*

***

But was "Wet" where *Running Dry* truly began? Should I have led with my childhood, my parents, or the decade I spent trying (and failing) to sell my work before breaking through with that one for *Future Sex Magazine?*

Pulling at my once-black-now-white beard and rubbing my   previously-outrageously-maned-now-thoroughly-bald-head and realizing I only have so much space—and you have only so much patience—let's jump to (or would it be back?) to why I've constantly strived to push myself creatively.

There's a pragmatic aspect to it, of course, as while there is nothing wrong with only doing what you love, it also tends to limit the number of books, magazines, and sites you can write for.

More importantly, you'll never know what you're good at until you try. My own scorecard is littered with plenty of hits and an overabundance of misses. Erotica worked, scriptwriting not so much; so far, so good, with non-fiction; poetry…better left unsaid.

Surprisingly, my LGBTQIA2S+ fiction was a hit. But it, too, had to start somewhere. Specifically when Michael Thomas Ford, another "Glamorous Nerd Pornographer," invited me to submit to *Best Gay Erotica 1995*.

As flattered as I was nervous (at least not terrified), I asked him…if it was, um, er, ah, okay since I wasn't (ahem) gay.

Michael, bless his sweet soul, replied with, "Go for it." My story, "Stroke The Fire," was accepted and went on to be in Richard Labonté's *Best of Best Gay Erotica*.

Since then, I've written a lot, and I mean a lot of queer fiction, both erotic and otherwise, and as long as my work generates smiles and not frowns, I don't ever want to stop.

That answers how I became a writer of LGBTQIA2S+ fiction but not why my novels and stories have (so far) been well-received. In case you're wondering, I've never lied to editors, publishers, or readers about my age, gender, ethnicity, or sexual orientation.

Pondering, pondering some more, continuing to ponder, and pondering until I can't remember what "pondering" means, I eventually came to the conclusion I've done as well as I have by focusing not on our differences but what our commonalities; how sex can be awkward, disappointing, embarrassing, and still really hot; what it feels like to be an outsider; to want to be desired and, more than anything, to be loved.

Not to make light of the LGBTQIA2S+ community's struggle to be accepted, recognized, respected, and treated as fellow human beings, but I tried to bring the same sympathy and understanding to Doud as a gay man as well as a vampire when "Wet" evolved into *Running Dry*.

***

Another imagination exercise I've developed is to reflexively deconstruct whatever I'm watching, reading, listening to, etc.— immediately followed by getting a kick out of making it my own.

Vampires were (are) no exception. Initially terrified at the prospect of writing a (sigh) vampire story, my brain soon buzzed with playful possibilities—above which circled a pair of fundamental ideas:

If vampires are essentially apex predators, what sort of…if not people, then persons would they be? Not, I decided aristocratic, debonair, or in any way, shape, or form cool and/or collected.

Powerful? For sure. Scary? Definitely. Unlike how vamps are usually depicted as supremely powerful, seductively alluring creatures with a romantic dash of haunting tragedy, Doud would be the opposite: crippled with guilt, neither refined nor wealthy, and whose predatory instincts are as horrific as they are inescapable.

Not to mention desperately lonely, and as with everyone, everywhere, he's made painful, occasionally monstrous mistakes—as another frequent vamp trope is, despite their bloody diet regimen, lots of people are willing to die to become one.

Put yourself in the vamp's coffin: Are you a partner, a lover, a person—albeit an undead one—to them, or merely a fang-toothed means to an end? What does it feel to be the former, and if it's the latter, what do you do about it…and them?

Now add one hundred years of failure, guilt, and shame. To make things extra interesting, suicide isn't an option; try, and my vamp's body would take over, drinking as many people as necessary to recover.

Having fun? Strange as it may seem, I was! Though more was yet to come. No cape and cowl, stakes and holy water, coffin sleeping or night prowling for Doud—or even a pair of fangs.

To feed, he'd instead lock his horribly distended mouth over the victims' and brutally suck them dry, leaving only a handful of dry bones and a few clumps of hair behind.

"Wet" flowed straight from my burbling imagination and into (onto?) Microsoft Word—with Thomas and Michael Rowe's acceptance of it for their anthology as the icing on its bloody frosted cake.

Though to what would probably be Doud's immortal displeasure and my unending delight, this "vampire" would rise again.

***

Of the dozens of publishers I've worked with, I'll always have a soft spot for the late, lamented Alyson Books. Specializing in LGBTQIA2S+ fiction, it was one of the big three (or so) companies that fueled the '90s erotica boom.

I worked, more or less, with all of them, but Alyson felt like home. From one editor to another—crying my eyes out when a favorite went on to greener pastures—my work was encouraged and appreciated.

Dirty Words, my first LGBTQIA2S+ collection and Lambda Literary Award Finalist, was with Alyson. Together with doing my own anthologies for them, my stories also routinely appeared in ones by many of their other editors. Sometimes several times in the same book—which was why they asked me to use Beth Greenwood or Alice Blue in addition to my usual M.Christian pseudonym.

Back then, short stories and I were old chums: give me a theme, erotic or not, when you want it, and how much you'll pay, and faster than you can say, "literary streetwalker with a heart of gold," I'd give you what you want.

Novel writing was another thing entirely; if the thought of submitting something to a gay vampire anthology scared the tomato juice out of me, the idea of writing 60,000 words was a nightmare.

I needed a confidence booster, someone to say, "I know you can do it,"—exactly what my editor at Alyson Books told me.

But what to write? Along with a bouquet of roses and a heartfelt thank you card, I asked my favorite editor that very thing.

As you probably guessed, his response was, "You can't go wrong with vampires."

***

A lot had changed between *Sons Of Darkness* and working on *Running Dry*. Not to spoil anything, but Doud's shtick in "Wet" was painting portraits of his victims using their regurgitated bodily fluids.

Fine and/or dandy for 1996 though it wasn't very long before DNA evidence gathering was everywhere. Originally a "what the hell do I do now?" moment, I light-bulbed Doud suddenly lacking a coping mechanism was what he and the book needed to double down on his already complicated existence.

It was a thrilling, intimidating, frustrating, and often depressing book to write. Still, between bursts of giddy exuberance and bouts of crippling self-doubt, I somehow managed to get it done—and, to my great relief, mixed with no small amount of anxiety, Alyson Books published it in 2006.

Am I happy with it? Though I'm mostly and only occasionally a smidgen less proud of everything I write, *Running Dry* is special.

From my years penning queer fiction to the invitation to submit to *Sons Of Darkness*, and from there the encouragement to turn "Wet" into a fully-fledged novel, *Running Dry* is a reminder everyone deserves to be accepted, recognized, respected, and if not loved then at least really liked—including myself.

***

Twenty years and five other novels (with three more in the works) later, I'm beyond blessed the beyond-awesome folx at Queen Of Swords Press have released this special edition of *Running Dry.*

Because if vampires are anything, they, and hopefully the readers who like to read about them and the writers who like to write about them, will be around for a *very* long time.

—*M.Christian, 2025*

M.CHRISTIAN

RUNNING DRY

PREFACE

Hollywood, 1916

"They say the seas are going to dry up. Blow away."

"I've heard that."

"The moon, too. It's going to leave, sail off into the sky. Leave us behind," Sergio said, swinging his feet off the edge. First the left, then the right, dancing with the heights. "Do you think we'll see that?"

"We could," Doud said, arm around Sergio's shoulders. To reassure him, and to remind himself that this was real, firm and solid, he tugged him closer.

Mahogany eyes directed at him, Sergio said, "Everyone will get old, turn to dust. But we'll still be here, won't we? The earth will be like the desert. No oceans, no water, no one will be alive. But we'll still be here." His legs stopped swinging.

"Maybe. Other things could happen, too. You never know for sure. Time changes too much." Sitting on the toes of rearing elephants, they looked down on the gleaming architecture of Babylon, a plaster movie set, brilliantly white from a still neighborly moon.

Despite the height, Doud wasn't afraid. Not of falling, at least. He knew the elephants Sergio had made for Mr. Griffith, believed in his lover's craftsmanship, and implicitly trusted them to carry their weight. He hoped he knew Sergio as well, but he was still quietly grateful for the simple strength of his sculpture. Men were too complex, too unpredictable. Apparent solidity and dependability all too often hid deep flaws. The elephants of *Intolerance*, though, were wood and plaster.

Dependable wood, trustworthy plaster.

"Ever been to the desert?" Sergio asked unexpectedly. "I went there, with some friends, just after I came here. Hot, like a stove. But I didn't think of cooking, the kitchen, or food, only that it was like a line across a page, like the start of a drawing. Now, I think of it like the way the world will be. All boiled away—just hot air and that line." Drawing his hand across the horizon, he underlined distant Hollywood.

"Too hot and dry for me. But we can go sometime. Both of us." He didn't need to say *we have lots of time*.

"They say the war will end soon. The War to End All Wars— but that's not true, eh? We'll find out, I guess."

"It'll end. They always do." Doud tried to catch his attention again, but the other man refused to look away from the bright lights of the distant city.

"Even our Babylon will be gone. Mr. Griffith's film is over. They'll break up my elephants."

"There'll be other pictures. You'll see."

After a moment of tense silence, Sergio's gaze swung back to Doud. "You'll be there, won't you?"

"I will," Doud replied, gently stammering, delicately hesitant. *I will*: not a promise, just desire. With it, abrupt reality on the toes of great white elephants: *please, let this one work out. I don't want to kill him.*

"Kiss me," Sergio said, closing those dark marble eyes.

And Doud did, a simple kiss on the edge of a Hollywood eternity.

CHAPTER I

Los Angeles, 1993

P*EOPLE WILL PAY A fortune for crap*, Shelly thought—certainly not for the first time, absolutely not for the last—*but the trick is to be* happy *selling crap.*

Taking another drag, she took a long, leisurely, moment to relish the smoke. A dozen or so Polaroids were splashes of color on her green glass and black steel desk. One of them was trapped under her *Bitch is Back* coffee mug, but she didn't tug it free. *Awful,* looking down at the spread, tapping each with a filter tip*: ugly, piece of shit, hideous, crap, bullshit. A loser's hand: talentless high, failures wild.*

Deal me out. Tilting back, she blew a long, sinuous stream of steel gray towards the distant ceiling. *Should just buy the lot; hang them on the walls and watch the money come rolling in. Pay the rent here, pay off the mortgage at home, kill the credit cards, and eat out—a lot.* Looking up from the ugly colors, she focused first on the gallery, and then on through the front windows. Saturday morning Los Angeles drove by, out and about on Melrose: fit, hip, tanned and successful. *Come on assholes, get your trendy Stairmaster asses in here and buy hideous junk.*

Another thought, again not for the first, or the last, time. *What the hell am I doing?* She wasn't a kid anymore, but at 40 was still a few years away from rocking on a porch somewhere. Sure, she wasn't a beauty, but then she never had been: dark brown curls over a pair of amber eyes set a little too deep in her face. Nice nose above an expressive mouth, quick to smile—or to sneer. Body of curves, (when she was being polite with herself), a little chubby when she wasn't. She may not have been called beautiful, but she was called fun, mouthy, a wicked broad, and other things that had made her playful lips curl into an even brighter grin.

Back to the spread: the blue and gold one, all streaks, splatters and blurs. The illicit love child of Pollack and DeKooning. It wasn't hideous, just bad. *Winner by default.* Flipping the shot over, she scanned the name and phone number scrawled on the back in hurried purple ballpoint. *Today's your lucky day.*

Propping the blue and gold shot against an unopened box of business cards, she grabbed her sleek, Italian-designed phone. People might pay millions for crap, but she didn't want to sell crap. What she wanted was to feel good about what she did, like actually selling something worth more than the paint and canvas. That's what she believed she wanted, at least when she had enough in her bank account for the rent, the mortgage, the bills, and eating out.

Phone in hand, cool hum of a dial tone in her ear, the door opened to the cough of unseasonable Santa Ana air. For a second, the air conditioning fought the invading atmosphere before winning, transforming nose bleeding dryness into temperate store ambiance.

"Good afternoon," she said long before glancing up from the periwinkle blue enameled ashtray she was grinding her cigarette into. "Give a holler if you need anything."

When she was riding the buzz of a good day she'd spice it up a bit: "Looking for anything in particular?" or "Have a blank wall that needs something?" but she wasn't, so she didn't. Too many during the last few days had wandered in just to glance around, frown, step out, or simply steal a few quick lungfuls of AC.

Still, Mrs. Mankowitz's daughter always tried to put on a polite face, even if the woman inside wanted to snap, growl, or yell out coiled-spring frustration. Besides, even with rent and mortgage paid, credit cards down to four digits, and a dinner out in the near future, a sale was still a sale. So what if it was a piece of crap, and the buyer an idiot with too much money and no taste?

Objects D was just a twenty foot wide, forty foot long space, door to bathroom and storeroom in back, big windows in front, so she didn't need to twist or turn to see him. Tall (damned tall), dark (swarthy but not black), and handsome (but not pretty). Good nose, great eyes, muscles but not on muscles. Just enough. Long dark hair simply shampooed, virgin, never fucked with by a stylist, and gripped by a cheap hair band into an unfashionably long ponytail. Simple burgundy (like *Bistro vin ordinaire*), cotton shirt, modestly buttoned despite the hot day. Black jeans, showing pale scuff zones of everyday wear. Work boots, but not Doc Martens or some style-of-the-moment, footwear. *Too clean and sharp to be a Working Joe, too rough and casual to be a player. Arty contractor? Successful (hahahaha) artist? Biz grunt. Set designer? Production Supervisor? A director? Maybe, but only of commercials.*

Craned forward, he was examining a Lavelle print, one of her favorites. Not perusing, not scanning, not peering. Really, honestly, *looking* at it, which added a tug of sincerity to her professional grin. It'd been too long since anyone had seen what she was offering, most of the AC thieves just cruising for matches to new, ten thousand dollar Helten sofas, or Sedia sectionals.

Making sure her smoke was out so the smoldering, embarrassing carcinogens didn't screw up the deal, she stood, then rounded her slab of thick glass and industrial tubing. *Calm down girl. Don't come on too strong*, was her thought, even though she was buoyantly eager. It was something she hadn't felt in a long time, a novel emotion. She knew, just knew, that he wasn't going to ask if she had a 'picture' with a 'peachy yellow, and a flare or two of gold' in it.

Still, she couldn't resist letting a little of her excitement leak through some climbing octaves. "That's one of my favs. Really. Great use of color, and I just adore the energy. Makes me feel better just looking at it."

"I like it." With obvious effort, he turned from the lines and color, large, dark eyes staying with the print until the last possible instant. When they left and his gaze floated to Shelly, his smile grew. "But I'm searching for something in particular."

"Just let me know what you want, and I'm sure I can get it for you." She fought a wince. *Christ, how much more desperate can I sound?*

"Thank you." His face was long, classical, his mouth full and expressive. His voice gently musical. The "ou" especially sounded like the closing note to an aria, gently melodious in a city known for crisp, brittle sentences. LA didn't speak: it had meetings, appointments, interfaces. He didn't speak, he sang. "I'm trying to track down an artist. I don't see any of his things here, but I think you had him in here a while ago. He worked in lots of heavy reds. Portraits. Odd texture, too." The last while rubbing thumb and forefinger together, trying to recall the exact feeling.

Mentally flipping Polaroids, she murmured a thoughtful "Humm…" Not on the walls was a problem. Occasionally waiters and valets became artists, but artists who slipped back into the steady income of waiters and valets rarely came back. Eating regularly killed more young creative types than starvation.

*Heavy reds. Portraits…*her internal catalog of painters and paintings stopped. *Oh, crap.* "Doesn't ring any bells. Sorry," she lied, walking back to her desk. "But let's poke around and see what I can turn up."

"I hope you can find him," he said, as she knelt down in front of her stubby little two-drawer filing cabinet. "Got a production starting, and I think he'd be perfect."

Yanking open the stubborn top drawer, the precarious stack of exhibition catalogs and calendars on top threatening to topple, she tried to cover her nerves with prattle. "That's wonderful! Well, if we can't find who you're thinking of, I'm sure I can point you to someone just as good."

"I'm sure you could, but I'm interested in just this one for now."

Reaching in, she grabbed a thick, blue rubber-banded stack of shots. Snapping the band free, she nervously shuffled them, pretending to glance at the colors as they flashed by. "If he was in here then he's…well, in here." Shuffle, shuffle: sketches, a mosaic, parodies of advertising art, even some classic Vargas-style pinups. "So what kind of production are you working on?" He wasn't in the pile she was dealing onto the desk, he was in another, in the bottom drawer, but she wasn't going to tell him that.

Flipping through the images, she felt his eyes sweeping over each one, hunting a certain color, a special media.

"Oh…a horror film. Werewolves, I think." A gentle chuckle. "I can't keep them straight anymore. I'm just on set design, advising on title work. If you can find the one I'm thinking of, I think he'd he perfect." Discomfort dulled his face, and he seemed to lose focus, gazing at her hands pinching and flipping the photos, but not at the photos themselves. "I think I remember his name, if that helps."

Her laughter came out staged. Badly acted. "Absolutely! You name him and I've got him."

"Doud, that was his name. Do you know how to reach him?"

Crap. Better fess up. "Oh, yeah…that's right, I remember him now, he had a little show here, a year or so ago. Portraits, like you said. Got some good press, too, considering how weird his medium was. Cow blood." She staged a shudder before standing back up. "Disturbing stuff. Perfect for a horror movie."

"Yes, that's him. Do you know how to reach him? It's really important." The music in his voice was all of a sudden crammed with violins; sharp, tense notes.

"Hate to say it, but I don't. He had that small show here, and that was it. Too bad, too, he was something else. Lots of great stuff. But that was it. He was only here for a few weeks, and then he just came in, took it all down, and walked out. Never really said why. Really disappointing. I thought he really could have gone somewhere."

"Do you have any idea where he is? An old address, or phone number? I really need to locate him. We go into production very soon. Could be great exposure. Money, too, of course." All this with a grin that was a bit too wide, muscles too tight at the corners.

"I'm sorry. He left a number, but the last time I called, it was disconnected. Too damned bad, really. Like I said, the guy had promise. Tell you what, why don't I ask around? A lot of the artists hang out together. You'd be surprised who knows who around here."

"Thank you. Like I said, I need to find him." From a back pocket, he pulled out a thick leather wallet and extracted a business card. "If you find out anything, anything at all, give me a call. That's my cell number."

She glanced at the name, the title (Production Artist) and knew where the music in his voice came from: Vivaldi, Albinoni,

Mascagni, Boccherini. One number, no address. "I will. Sure thing."

"I hope so. I really need to find him." Tension in his long body, dark eyes narrowed. "It's very important."

"Gotcha. Hey, while you're here, let me show you some other artists who might work for your project. Take this guy, for instance…" she said, gesturing at a massive acrylic, a great molten wave of brilliant color, bursting from a cartoonish crayon factory, bulbous walls split like ruptured organs.

"Not as interesting. But if you find Doud, call me immediately. If you don't mind, I'll be back tomorrow to see if you've had any luck."

Then he was gone: door opened, door closed. Burning Santa Ana sweeping in, then gone, Shelly's goosebumps never leaving her bare forearms.

CHAPTER 2

E VEN THOUGH HE WASN'T hungry, he walked back into the kitchen to the fridge, and took a brief inventory. A jar of pickles, half-full. The remains of a broiled chicken from the local chain store wrapped in foil. A brown-crusted pot of mustard he should throw away. Same with the horseradish. Other things, scanned too fast, just registered as *no, no, no.* Then: peanut butter.

It was getting toward late afternoon, the time when the lowering sun splashed through the window right over his head, a blinding glare. Closing his eyes, he opened a drawer by feel, reached in among the tarnished silverware and felt around, cautious of the few sharp knives, until his thumb rolled into a spoon. Facing into the warm light, he performed a practiced little domestic ballet: spoon caught between two fingers of the hand wrapped around the cool glass of the peanut butter jar, other hand, a good grip on the lid. Good hard twist. Lid on the counter by the empty drying rack, next to the sink full of dirty dishes. Spoon in a twisting scoop, and even though he wasn't that hungry, he sucked on a fat glob of sweet, salty peanut butter.

Jar in hand, spoon a metal pacifier, he padded back through the apartment. The day was hot, and even though he'd suffered through six long years of LA heat waves in the place, a big change from San Francisco, he kept most of the windows closed. It was how he felt: dark, shaded, and silent.

It was also what he'd been called. His eyes were large, but seemed to be always staring past you, out at an unknown horizon, in a hawkish, could-be-called Middle Eastern face attached to a rather flat head. Black hair, always with a faint sheen of richness, that would twist into Grecian curls—if he ever let it get that long. He looked like he was in his middle to late 40s. He wasn't.

Past the living room full of heavy dark furniture. Past the bedroom with the massive bed with its mahogany posts. The dresser with the straight-razor and pearl-handled hairbrush. Not for the first time, he thought about changing, hiring some red-cheeked kid to come in and change it all, maybe go back to modern and streamlined, or at least update himself to the '50s. It was also about time for a new place, maybe a bungalow, or something with rounded corners and glass brick. Those were good years after all, at least for him. But even if he was tired of the hefty wood, the dull-colored rugs, the crystal he never used, he knew he wouldn't change.

Later, when he felt a bit better about everything, he might move yet again. A new apartment, maybe even a new city. He had money, careful savings and investments from long years painting signs, working as a draftsman, and even selling some art. Then he'd gotten into buying and selling houses. He'd done a lot of that. The problem wasn't the expense, it was just too much work to think about. But even as he enjoyed his peanut butter, he knew he'd have to start thinking about it, and soon. He'd been in LA for almost six years. Couldn't stay in one place for too long.

Still sucking his spoon, Doud stood in the doorway to the spare bedroom, his studio. No curtains here, nothing dark or ponderous. No curtains at all, in fact, just clean (more accurately, just dirty) windows, with a view of the silver flashes, reflections, of the traffic on Sunset Boulevard. Bare hardwood floor. A metal stool. An easel. A plastic cart from an art supply store, with stiff, stubborn, wheels, the top a deli counter of jars—many still with their olive, pickle, mustard, horseradish, and even peanut butter labels—all full of brushes, knives, and various shades of brown water. Perched precariously on the side, a brand new box of charcoals.

On the good easel, a canvas. On the canvas, a few streaks of gray and black, the first strokes towards a portrait in a new medium.

Loudly sucking his spoon, he stared at it, hoping the painting would get better. But it didn't. It wasn't working. It wasn't the same.

Never looking away from the canvas, he put his jar down on the cart. When his blind hunt for a clean space produced only musical chimes of full, half-full, and empty glasses, he balanced the peanut butter jar carefully on the windowsill.

The man's face was there, hanging clearly in his mind. The man from the night before. The man from that working class bar in Van Nuys. A roofer, he'd said he was. Between jobs. After a few beers, they'd stumbled out of that sad little dive in the middle of the night, and for the first time he'd really seen him under the hard, merciless white of a streetlight. Skin the same brown as his bedposts. Tanned, but glowing, as if lit by harsh fires deep inside. Hard eyes, mean eyes. He knew exactly how he wanted to capture him. The cant of his head; the shape of his skull; his plump, almost fat, lips; his darker-than-black, curly hair. The memory of his face hovered, ghostly, at the end of Doud's outstretched fingers.

He knew that if he didn't get his portrait just right, he'd never be able to get rid of that ghostly image, the incomplete painting hovering somewhere just out of the corner of his sight.

Never get rid of the guilt.

Picking up the charcoal again, he rolled it in his fingers, watching, hypnotized by the ashen dark that spread across the whorls of his fingertips. Some artists, he knew, actually got their fingers into their art, reaching in and spinning their fingers across their medium. He hadn't tried that yet. Doubted he would. It was just too primitive, too basic, too big a step away from the mind, too small a step from the trees, the African savanna.

Not that the old way, how he used to work, was refined, but at least it was *personal*. Touching the canvas would be passionate, yes, but it would necessitate his fingers slipping and sliding against the weave of the canvas. That was too much Doud, not enough *subject*. Not like the way he used to work. Direct, life to canvas, straight route from inspiration to medium. Capturing their lives.

Not anymore. Now it was charcoal, at least for today, just as it'd been oils, watercolors, and acrylics before. Tomorrow a collage, or even a damned fresco for all he knew. But he couldn't go back.

Practicing in the air, drawing imaginary charcoal streaks, he tried to visualize the way the dark, crumbly, powdery stuff would behave as he put it against the canvas. Stroke there, his eyes, stroke there, his lips, stroke there, his neck, stroke there, his teeth, filling in the ghostly likeness hanging in front of him. That part was easy.

Getting the new materials to behave and follow what he wanted to create, that was the hard part.

Anger, like the sun peaking suddenly over a building, blinded him. Hot urges: throw the dirty stick at the wall, snap the canvas frame in half, sweep it across all the pickle, horseradish, and peanut butter jars to create a primitive, visceral wave of just plain ugly water.

Deep breath, out in a long sigh. Even if he could capture him, hold his face exactly, precisely, down on the tightly woven fabric, it wouldn't be the same. The image of him would be there, but what had been important about him wouldn't be. A picture would always be just a picture, but a painting—the way he used to do it, the way that felt right and natural —was an exchange. The man he'd talked to in that little bar, the man he'd walked out with might be dead, but his portrait, and a bit of his life and essence, would always be there.

At least that's how it should be.

How can you say *thank you*, and even *I'm sorry*, with just charcoal on a stretched sheet of muslin?

Should he go back? That was an option, but the idea scared him. Even if he painted just for himself as he used to, burning it as soon as he finished, pouring the ashes down the sink or flushing them down the toilet, it would still be too easy to make a mistake. A part not burned, a bit not ruined enough by water. Evidence left behind of his crimes.

Give it all up? Admit to the world what he was, step out into the hard, unforgiving sunlight? Not a lot stayed with him as he traveled. Not his apartments, furniture, nothing really that was personal or intimate. But he did have time, years, decades. Momentum. Habits die hard, especially the habit of living.

Picking one of his favorite brushes from a pickle jar, he rubbed his charcoal smudged fingers along its length, relishing its silky fineness. It felt good to hold it, like walking down a safe street, reading a familiar book. Relaxing. He grinned as he twirled it, appreciating its balance.

Memory, then: the coarse, rough man punching him in the neck. Doud falling, clammy pavement suddenly grinding across his artists' fingertips. The man kicking, steel-toed boots breaking Doud's ribs.

All because Doud had asked the roofer for *"A kiss. Just a kiss."*

It was a game he'd played before, of course. Ask for some-thing nice and sweet and innocent and when they punched or kicked in response, it would be permission for Doud to take what he needed. Later he would think of it as self-defense, as protecting himself. Though that was a lie. It was nothing but an excuse. The roofer was never a threat.

After punches to his face and, after he fell to the ground, boots to his ribs, Doud had gotten up, and moved. Moved as only he could. Then he'd taken his kiss.

A kiss goodbye.

Anger didn't matter, justification didn't matter. Doud owed him, but had no way of repaying the debt.

So familiar, so practiced, even though it'd been many months since he'd last painted an honest, and forgiving, portrait, Doud worked the brush some more, until it had a neat, perfect, tip. Sitting on his stool, he tilted his head back and opened his mouth. He then pushed what remained of that roofer up the shaft of his throat. Warm, wet, full, the sensation made him smile despite the solemnity of the occasion. When he felt it rise to the back of his throat, he took the brush and dipped it into the reser-voir. A pause, as the fluid soaked into the hairs, then out, past his teeth, past his face and back down to the easel, the canvas. Wet and red, he held the brush above the surface.

It would feel so good. It would feel wonderful. It would feel *right*: a way of giving back what he'd taken with a single, hard kiss. One stroke, then another. A painting done. Just a little blood. A pint, maybe more. Doud would barely miss it, especially since he'd taken so much from the roofer.

But that part of his life was over. It wasn't safe anymore. It was that simple. He'd just have to find another way.

Plunging the dull red brush in the paint-brown water, he swirled it around angrily, washing it all away. Withdrawing it once, twice, three times, examining the head each time, even squeezing it between his fingers, he made sure only water and old paint oozed out. When it was clean, he wiped it on a rag and replaced the brush, with some solemnity, back among the others.

Then, a sound trickled into his consciousness, irritating and persistent. Harsh and mechanical. The phone. The damned phone.

Shouldn't answer it. He rarely gave out his number, often thinking he should just have the phone disconnected. Still, it was a break, something to get him away from his studio, even just to hang up on a telemarketer.

Frowning, he walked down the hall, wiping his hands reflexively on his stiff studio towel, past the even darker bedroom, towards the setting sun brilliant in the kitchen, taking a hard right into the cool darkness of his living room. Modern, his phone was an infernal device, full of functions and features that still confused him, despite his having owned it for more than a year. "Hello?" he snapped into the receiver.

"Doud? It's Shelly." Static, and cars roaring by, told him she was using the building intercom, wired to his phone. "God, I hate these things. Can you hear me? Listen, I had this guy come into the shop today asking about you. I thought you might want to know. He said he had work for you, but he was kind of weird. Buzz me in. I feel like a moron yelling into this thing."

Even though she was a friend, he didn't move to buzz. People would sometimes ask questions, friends always did, which was why he avoided contact with the first, and rarely had the second. Shelly, though, was an exception. Although confused, and even angered, by his request to pull his paintings down from her gallery, she'd never questioned his decision. It was pleasant to know someone who didn't want to dig up what he wanted to keep buried.

There was more than that, but what he couldn't exactly say, making him hesitate even longer. When he had friends he usually ended it, or simply vanished, after ten years or so. Longer than that and questions became suspicions, like why Doud didn't age. But Shelly was brusque, chain-smoking, sometimes demanding, and always wonderfully alive. For Doud, with blood seeping into every day of his very long life, being around someone who existed in a perpetual present, who accepted him as just a gay man with a few quirks, was freeing. And nothing else. With her, he didn't have to be alone in his painful and lonely life, when he was with her he could almost forget it all, become a simple companion in her loud and raucous life.

And she was waiting downstairs.

Cursing inaudibly, he glanced down at his fingers, relieved that they were clean, the towel free of incriminating red. "Okay!" he yelled into the phone, jamming a finger down on the 9 button to release the door. The rag was tossed back towards the studio, landing on the floor.

A knock at the door, loud and strong. There in a few steps, he undid the chain, pulled back the bolt and jerked it open. Red cheeks even redder than usual, brown curls slightly limp. "Hi, hon," she said bending in to peck him on the cheek before he could say anything. "So glad you're around. God, what a nightmare getting over here. Traffic's a mess."

"That's awful," was all Doud could think of saying, getting out of her way as she rushed in. He closed and locked the door behind her. Even though he resented the intrusion, especially as she'd almost caught him with blood on his brush, it was good to see her.

"Anyway, what I came over for. This guy comes into the shop asking about your stuff. Now I know what you said before, about not painting again and not to even ask you about it, but this guy really seemed interested. Really interested. Could mean money, I guess, but there was something else about him. Kind of intense. Knew your name, which is weird if you ask me, considering that scrawl you used to put on your work."

Her bringing up his paintings wasn't a good thing. "Thank you very much, Shelly, but I'm not working anymore. Like I told you."

"I remember, but I wanted to come by anyway just to give you his card. He's in 'the biz,' so who knows where this could lead? Bucks, but maybe an in-road, too. Wouldn't it be great to see your stuff up there on the screen?"

The idea filled Doud with dread. "Yes…I guess it would, but I really have given up."

Standing in the shadowy, narrow hall, she leaned towards the living room, too polite to just go in and sit down, but obviously wanting to. It was one of the things he liked about her, that her broad and laughing self was always being restrained by an almost prim sense of social niceties. It made him relax around her, knowing that this leash would always keep her from acting out. "I'm sorry to hear that. Like I've told you, I think you've got something really special. I'm not bullshitting you. I wouldn't do that. Not to you, anyway."

Even though having his friend there was a relief, he had things to deal with. Like thanking a roofer for his liquid life. He may not like the medium, but it was something he had to learn to do. "I appreciate that," he said, damning himself for automatically relocking the door. Reaching up for the bolt, he dug out a spontaneous excuse: "I'm sorry to be rude, but I'm not feeling that well. I should get to bed. I hope you'll understand."

"Oh, gee, I'm so sorry, honey! I'll head off then, no problem. Like I said, just wanted to let you know about this guy. He said he was going to come by tomorrow and see if I could get a hold of you. I'll just let him know that you're not interested. Or if you'd rather, you could just give him a call, let him know yourself. He was kinda weird, but you know, who in this town isn't? Anyway, I'd better get out of here then, and leave you to your chicken soup."

"I'll be fine. Just need some sleep," he said, only partially feigning weariness. "Dinner sometime?" he added, feeling guilty for shoving her out the door.

"That'd be grand! I heard about this great little Italian place on La Brea that I'd love to try. Deal?" Heading out the now open door, she readjusted her embroidered purse. Passing, she pecked his cheek again.

"Sure—that'd be fun." Beginning to close the door, her hand on the jamb stopped him short.

"Damn, I'd forget my tits if they weren't nailed on. Here's that guy's card. Like I said, he promised to come by to see if I'd got to you. If you want to meet him, just swing by sometime tomorrow, or you can give him a call."

"I'll think about it," he said, taking the card.

"See you later, hon. Hope you feel better."

After waving her down the hall towards the elevator, locking up for the night, again, he finally looked at the card. In the dim light of his front hall he could just make out the simple serif letters: *Sergio Insana.*

Hands back to the chain, fighting the stubborn links, the catch, the bolt, the door. Then he was running down the hall, yelling her name as loud as he could.

CHAPTER 3

"So," Shelly said, arms folded tight, body tense, "you're kidnapping me. Is that it?"

Next to them in traffic was a pickup, the driver looking tired and deflated, head a balding mass of sagging skin and heavy wrinkles. Through the dust on the truck door, Doud could see the name of a popular exterminator company.

"Just want to know for sure. Never been kidnapped before. Don't really know what it's supposed to be like." The window had been down. but the choking cloud began to filter in. In response, Shelly leaned a finger on a button, whirring the window closed.

"Shelly…" Doud, behind the wheel of his Lexus, started, but then stopped. After a few seconds he simply asked, "You don't believe me?"

"I don't believe anything right now. My poor ol' brain's rattling around in here like a dried up apricot in a coffee can." She tapped a temple with the filter end of an unlit Camel. Doud didn't like people smoking in his car. That she hadn't asked meant something to him. What that was, he didn't know. Familiarity? Maybe, that despite all of this, a part of her had stayed his friend.

"The photos," he said, watching the traffic rather than her. They'd been driving for half an hour and only gone a few miles. "I showed you my pictures."

Tearing down the four flights, he'd caught up with her in the lobby. Hand tight around her upper arm, he'd led her back into the elevator, up, and back into his apartment. Then his questions, which she'd responded to first with friendly laughter, but then with serious, much more complete answers.

"But you *are* kidnapping me, right? Taking me somewhere I don't want to go. That's what they call it, isn't it?"

His questions answered, hers began. But he'd refused to answer, until he'd gotten her seated on his vast green sofa.

"Yeah, I saw your photos, Doud. Like I said—" unlit cigarette to head again, tap, tap, tap—rattle, rattle, rattle. "Maybe you've got one of those Photoshop computers in your bedroom. A little presto, some change-o, and there you are in your knickerbockers and straw hat in Hoboken, or wherever the hell that was supposed to be."

It was Brooklyn, in the summer. A cool, almost cold, summer: goosebumps at noon. Me in fine new clothes. Sean McCollin had just paid me to paint a sign: McCollin's Fine Clothiers for Gentlemen *in elegant, crisp typography. Goosebumps from more than the weather. I'd misspelled Glasgow in* Glasgow to New York. *He'd been so happy, proud of that sign, standing there with his thumbs in his vest, staring up at my work, unable to read a word of it.*

That was Papa, standing next to me. A few days before he caught me with that boy down the street. He broke my nose, kicked me out. Never saw Papa or Momma again. He, dead a year later when our house burned down, Momma—don't know what happened to her. He grimaced out at the freeway, not really seeing the cars.

A yellow and red ad on a bus begged Doud to advertise with the Yellow Pages. *Brooklyn in the summer.* One of five photos he'd kept. He hated photos, always refused to have them taken, always ducked the invitation, scowled at sudden flashes.

He had a good-sounding excuse to avoid any camera pointed in his direction. He was a professional artist, he'd lie, and so crystal lenses, emulsions, f-stops, were cheats: one button, one click, and there it was, untainted, exact and flawless reality, captured forever. With photography there was no interpretation, no examination, no personal view of anything except reality through a viewfinder.

Eternity without feeling, without the true, and horrible, complexities of living it.

"The pictures are real," was all he said, coming back to the moment. An SUV-full of kids, driven by a very tired, hollow-eyed mother, crawled next to them. One of the kids looked up, made a face. Doud pretended not to notice. The kid, no more than six, flipped him off.

"That's what *you* say. But then you would say that, wouldn't you?" Prowling through her small embroidered purse, she came up with a gold lighter, held it up to him with an inquisitive expression on her full, round, face. Silent question: May I light up?

"It's okay," he said with a weak, hopefully reassuring smile. "I don't mind."

"You're a prince," she said with gentle sarcasm, putting a blue and yellow flame to the tip of a cigarette. A long slow draw, seemed to settle her deeper into the passenger seat. "Want to know the truth? The real, honest, cross-your-heart-and-hope-to-die truth?" With that last she looked up at him, eyes wider than usual.

She continued. "I hope you're telling the truth. Really. I think that'd be cool. Like, maybe there really are monsters and were-wolves, and all that. The world wouldn't be so damned boring. But I just can't take it. It doesn't jive. What I should do, right now, is get out and run like hell." Puff, puff, puff. "Right, sure, I can just see it: 'Help, help, I'm being carjacked by a—'"

A car behind and to the left honked, loud and brassy. Jerking at the sound, Shelly's cigarette tumbled to the carpet. "Shit, shit, SHIT!" she said, stamping frantically. "Okay…okay, got it. Shit." Running a hand through her tangled hair, she unexpectedly laughed. "Crap…god, oh, crap, what a day, eh?"

Interruption halting his memory, bringing him back from where he wasn't ready to go, Doud grinned weakly at her.

"At least the carpet's okay," she said, picking up the mangled cigarette. Cradling it in her hand like a tiny, dead creature, she whirred the window down again. Traffic noise and exhaust washed in. Picking the cigarette off her palm, she flicked it out.

Reflexively, a new one came out, but she hesitated, lighter in her hand. She looked over at him, then the cigarette and her lighter went back into her bag.

He tried to concentrate on driving through the impenetrable traffic, but couldn't against the shame flushing, burning his dusky cheeks.

He'd seen her hands. They were shaking in fright.

CHAPTER 4

For the next half hour, a long, heavy, leaden silence was an unwelcome passenger in the car, sucking up the available air. Things to say spun in his mind, but nothing came out, the silence too oppressive, the momentum of not talking too great to overcome.

The sun was setting, throwing up crisp reflections off chrome and dirty glass from the other cars. Night suddenly seemed to come early, but was nothing but a semi rolling between them and the fat, red, setting sun. Then it was dawn again, a second illusion brought on by a glass-bottle water truck on the other side, dozens of shimmering, too bright mirrors and fractured rainbows, making Doud wince.

"Getting dark," Shelly observed, finally breaking the quiet, with it reclaiming a cigarette from her purse. "Crap. This is the worst I've ever seen it. We're going nowhere fast."

"It'll ease up soon," he croaked, voice rusty.

"Hey, it's broad daylight! How come you aren't burning up?" Suspicion laced her question, like she'd caught him in a lie.

No one had ever asked him that before. It felt odd to be compared to a character from the movies. "I like the sun. Sometimes it can get a bit bright, though." Another water truck followed the second, and he averted his eyes from the harsh glare.

"What about animals? Can you bite them?"

"I don't bite, and no, I can't. It's not the same."

"Seems like people would notice you, being old, but not looking it… What's up with that?"

"I don't stay long in one place. I keep moving."

"How did this happen to you? Were you bit or what?"

"It wasn't like that."

"Shit. This isn't making any sense." Scratching at a cheek, cold cigarette pinched between two fingers, she went on. "You sit me down, pull out some damned photos and tell me…well, hell, you tell me that you're fucking ancient, and that you have an old boyfriend in town, who I really shouldn't be around to meet. Then you force me into your car and we hit the damned road. Then you say you can go out anytime and get a suntan. What about garlic? What the hell do you have on your pizza? If you're going to play Dracula, at least get your story straight."

"You don't believe me? You said you did." He was exhausted, tired of talking, more tired of her not listening.

"I don't know, I can't figure this out. I like you, I really do. You know that. You're a friend. A good friend and I mean that. You're quiet, all moody and shit, you paint a damned great picture, and you're fun to go out with, but you've pulled the rug out. What's going on? Did you just have a meltdown and I'm just along for the ride? Take me home. Take me home or I'm going to start walking there myself."

"I can't."

"Sure you can. It's damned easy. It's called turning the wheel and taking your foot off the fucking gas. Anywhere will do."

Harsher and rougher with each second, her voice sounded like it was clawing up her throat. Seeing Shelly was to see Shelly angry. It was a part of her, as much as the easy smile and her machine-gun delivery, ten words when two would do. It normally was an act she put on when she was uncomfortable, or just bored, a hard-assed

New Yorker living in the land of fruits and nuts. Something normally reserved to be turned on other people. Doud didn't like being on the receiving end, especially when it came honestly, and not just performed on her public persona stage.

"I'm sorry. I can't." His own tones came out squeezed tight, forced down, locked up, key thrown away, words very carefully delivered. For him, it was always two words when ten were needed.

"Or what? You'll kill me? Suck my blood?" Even though he felt she was facing him, his eyes never wandered from the road or the other creeping machines on the freeway. "Screw you, Doud, screw you to hell. I'm getting out of here." Hand on the door handle, she was a pull away from bolting.

Then his hand was on her shoulder. Fast, too fast for anyone but Doud. One instant his fingers were resting on the wheel, the next they were wrapped around her blouse-shrouded muscles and bone. Too firm a grip, he knew, but he didn't let go.

"You can't go, Shelly."

"Why the hell can't I? Come on say something. I deserve an answer, right? Tell me what the fuck's going on."

Letting go, he pulled his arm back, and returned to concentrating on the irregular, glowing, pulsing heartbeats of stop-and-go traffic. After a few deep breaths, he said, "If you go, he might find you. If he finds you, he'll kill you." Saying more, explaining further, began to do something to his mind: flickering waves, roars and heavy weights, fury, anger, guilt, shame.

After a long, heavy moment, there was finally a flash of gold from her lighter. A small flame, then, held to a new cigarette, wavering in a very unsteady hand. Smoke soon shaded the car's interior soft gray. "Okay. Tell me."

"I knew Sergio a long time ago. We were…together. He's very dangerous. I just want to keep you safe."

After a moment of thought: "I can deal with that," she said, a shot of strength returning to her voice. "Had more than my fair share of loser boyfriends. But the rest of it? It's a bit much, you know? I'm not a good, logical woman. Never have been. Never will be. But I'm not an idiot, either. I trust you. I don't know why, not yet, but I do. You say get in the car, so I get in the car." She gestured with her cigarette, the tip a bright red arc.

Quiet again, measured in puffs and crawling traffic. "Doud?"

"Hmm?"

"Where are you taking me?"

"Barstow, or at least nearby. I have a house there."

"Have you had it long?"

"For…a while. It's big. It should still be in good shape. I haven't been there in five or six years."

"What does 'a while' mean, Doud? Even if I still don't believe a word you're saying, I want to know."

"1910," he said, realizing how long ago that sounded. Yesterday. It still felt like yesterday. He had no idea what those years, those decades must sound like to her.

"Bet real estate was real cheap back then," she said, turned away from him, looking out the window.

CHAPTER 5

"WHY DIDN'T YOU LIE to me? Why didn't you just tell me this old boyfriend of yours was an SOB, used to beat you up or something? I mean, I wouldn't necessarily accept him being a nasty son-of-a-bitch, but it's a helluva lot easier to take than learning he's some kind of monster, and, oh, by the way, so are you."

A monster. "I don't know." Traffic was still bumper-to-bumper, the sun now just a setting glow.

"It's just kind of weird, don't you think? Hell, you could have just grabbed me and said 'Let's do Vegas' and I'd have probably gone along. I'm always up for a quick adventure somewhere. Remember that John Waters festival in Santa Monica? Dinner one second, Divine eating dog crap the next." Pausing, she frowned at her shortening cigarette. "Then kidnapped."

The films had been ugly and disgusting, but he'd enjoyed their time together, her laughter contagious, even spreading to him.

He should have left her behind. Sergio might not come back to her gallery. A massive truck, like a thundering chromed bull, surged past on his right. Its headlights snapped on, matched by a string of decorative pin lights all along its sides. One moment a snorting beast, next a Christmas decoration.

Why did he tell her the truth? Putting himself back there, in the instant he read the name on that card, he tried to remember how he felt. Shock, absolutely, a cold water bath, but also a burning in his chest.

He'd been frightened.

That was it. So simple, and so stupid. He didn't want to be alone. He could have lied to her, he could have just told her that Sergio was a crazy ex-boyfriend and that she should close up, take a week off. Instead he'd opened the door and pulled her in.

Sergio, damn him to hell.

Other things had faded, vanished. Birthdays, other men, entire years in some cases, *gone.* But Doud still remembered that one night, perched at the feet of elephants, beholding the plaster brilliance of Mr. Griffith's Babylon. He even recalled the taste of the air: gypsum from the set, dust from the hills, garlic from their dinner, salty perspiration from his own nerves. He'd been wearing a pair of boots he'd gotten from a second-hand store, having ruined a good pair a few days before on the set. Paint and gypsum on good leather, cracking and flaking off, leaving behind stains that would never leave. Good leather in the morning, speckled and spotted with paint and plaster by noon.

Sneaking in, then, slipping by his consciousness, dreamy fantasy on tip-toes: Sergio by moonlight, sitting on the back steps of Doud's bungalow. The only place they could meet, because Sergio had been living with some of the other *Intolerance* craftsmen in a huge house in Pasadena. Sitting and smiling, smiling and laughing, sharing a bottle of red wine, listening to the crickets chirp their progressive concertos, looking at the stars, unreachably high over the flesh and blood celestials down in Hollywood. Between the sky and the city was the darkness of his dusty back yard, the profound black where it dropped away to brush and weeds far below. They'd just made love, their bodies still slick and salty, and, after a few minutes, they'd do it again.

He'd thought Sergio had been different, better than all the rest he'd transformed. The sculptor fresh off the boat, to whom Doud could show a whole new world. Through the young Italian everything had been incredible, a marvel, a wonder, and for a few months he'd even convinced himself that was how Sergio had been seeing him. That was until there was blood on Sergio's handkerchief, and Doud had realized that Sergio had been just like all the rest.

"Well, there's the problem," Shelly said. "Someone really fucked up."

Ahead, red and blue flashing lights in the dimming night. As he'd been driving, the lanes had converged. Now it was just two lanes out of five, three empty on the left, next to the center divider. Between the crawling cars and trucks, the bright red brilliance of flares on the asphalt. An accident. A bad one.

Just like all the others. Sergio hadn't understood what Doud had given him. Sergio had become a murderer, a monster. Furious, Doud now shoved crickets, salty sweat, and red wine from his mind.

Don't remember that. Remember this:

His bungalow, another night. A spaghetti dinner. Though Sergio worked wonders with plaster, paint, wood, and Doud's body, his hands lent no magic to food. More red wine. A cold night, too chilly for porch sitting. Doud had fired up his little heater, mixing the air with the sweet reek of gas, before lighting the stubborn old tin and brass thing with a safety match. Still too cold. Until it could warm up the house, they'd bundled against the foot of the bed, backs against the foot board, wrapped in one of Doud's scratchy Mexican blankets.

More flares in the present night. Red and blue twirling lights coming closer. They were in the farthest lane, but could see some of it between the other cars. Night had seriously arrived. All the cars were blazing with hard, white headlights. In his rear-view mirror, the horizon was lost against hundreds of bright glares. In front was a sea of similar, but smaller red lamps, occasionally brighter as people slowed to stare. Then, they'd kissed. Their last kiss. Doud hadn't wanted to, but he didn't have a choice. Sergio, like all the others, had to be stopped. Had to be killed.

During the first touch of lips to lips, Sergio's eyes had been soft and warm, obviously lost in the moment. Then Sergio's eyes had changed, bright with panicked understanding: Doud wasn't kissing out of love. It was, instead, a kiss of conclusion.

Trying to fight back, Sergio had hammered strong craftsman's fists against Doud's back. Bruises began, bones broke, but Doud's lips stayed tight, the seal between them absolute. Rough hands flailed, beating at Doud's head, until finally coming to his ears, gripping tightly.

Flailing, he'd pulled, tearing Doud's flesh from his skull.

Shaking his head, Doud tried to rid himself of the too-vivid memory, but some of it still managed to slip through: the pops and crackles of imbedded images, sounds, smells. Their lips tearing apart, a red geyser erupting from Sergio's mouth, splashing Doud with bathwater-warm brine and the taste of hot pennies.

Doud had roared in pain, hand flying to his ear, feeling the skin flopping off his head. The floor was covered in blood, some of it his own, most of it Sergio's. The back door banged open like a shot, as Sergio, shirtless, gleaming with spilled ocher, stumbled, weakened, dying, ran through it and off the low cliff, tumbling down into shaking scrub far below. Then an abrupt silence of frightened crickets.

"Doud? Doud? I'm getting hungry." Heavy machinery rolled by. Shelly paused until it passed. "Wanna get a bite somewhere? Bet we can find something halfway decent out here, wherever we are."

Following her gaze, he saw a gap in the traffic, a space between a creeping RV, and a gray-haired older man driving an immaculate antique sports car. Between them was shredded metal, black oil, glass flashing on concrete. An ambulance, rear door open, showing lights, IV bags, glowing instruments, a pair of paramedics leaning over someone on a gurney.

Not oil on the ground. Blood, in a splash of white light, the color of a sunset. A lot of sunsets.

"I'm not hungry. But I am tired. I'll pull over."

"Whatever you want is fine by me; high class or low rent. I'm not only easy, but I'm also cheap," she said. "It'll just feel good to stop for a while."

"We'll find a place for the night." The traffic had eased after the accident, and was now free flowing and fast. "Get a bite after." Lightheaded, he directed the heavy car towards the nearest off-ramp. Barstow was still many hours away, and it was getting late.

She giggled suddenly. "You know, I was just going to ask if you liked to eat, but I've been out to dinner with you lots of times. So what's the deal anyway? Is it like a dietary supplement or something? A vitamin?" As she laughed a bit more, he started looking for restaurants, motels. "Rich, nutritious, vitamin B, or O positive?"

"There's a place," he said, ignoring her, gesturing to an inexpensive chain. "After we check in, we can eat."

A signal stopped them. The town was small, low, but bright. Another extension of the gas station/strip mall/tract home spread of Los Angeles. Doud knew it had a name, something Spanish, but now it was just the outer edge of the spread. Probably only the people who actually lived or worked in it knew what it was really called. To everyone else, it was just a part of the larger whole.

"Sounds good to me. Food and getting my feet up will make me feel better. That or a really good fuck."

"I can help with two, but you're on your own with the third." The signal went from red to green, and they led the traffic down the brightly logoed avenue.

Her laugh was earthy and honest. "Thanks, I needed that. Nice to remember that you're a friend. Whoever or whatever you are."

CHAPTER 6

"TWO?" THE WAITRESS SAID, face pinched tight. Suspicion, or at least displeasure, loudly broadcast.

Message from her clearly received, Doud managed to say, "Yes, please." *Be polite.*

Shelly hadn't had such a diplomatic mother. "If it's not too much trouble."

The waitress led them to the back of the restaurant. "That's what I'm here for, hon," she said, not bothering to see if they followed.

After leaving them in a corner booth, she strolled off without bothering to ask if they wanted anything to drink. The buzzing fluorescents caught the greasy artwork, glaring ugliness stabbing his eyes as he cracked open his sticky bill of fare.

"Hey, Doud," Shelly said, gently drumming purple-lacquered nails on the back of his caramel-colored hand, "how about you make her a special, eh? Not that she looks tasty—"

"Please. Don't."

"I'm sorry, that was dumb. But I'm probably not dumb enough to be a *waitress!*" The last a stage whisper, directed at the front of the restaurant.

Shelly. An image of her: loud, rough, cigarette balanced between bright nails, a hoarse laugh, an elbow in the stomach, no matter how loud, how rough, how gaudy, a bright light there as well. As with so many times before, he felt his frustration fade. "No, I think you have to go to a special school for that."

Laughing, she covered her mouth with a cupped hand. "You're priceless."

Grinning, he returned to his menu. The lighting, the photos, the waitress, he'd felt the first, faint pang of hunger after checking into the motel, but after looking at the glossy, greasy images, those few pangs vanished into fuming disgust. Still, he knew he should eat. Ignoring his appetite, even when it was almost wiped out by nausea, wasn't a good idea. Craving one kind of food very often made him hungry for another kind of nourishment.

Thinking of that *other* need frightened him, but he still felt the warmth, the liquid, rolling and surging in his depths. Enough for a while anyway, if he kept it easy and avoided too much stress. A laugh started, squelched by faking a cough into a fist. *Sergio back there. Shelly right here. Not stressful, not at all.*

"God, you'd think they'd at least try to make this appetizing." Sigh. "Okay, girl, you have to pick *something*. There, that's it. I don't think even this place could screw up a Denver omelet. Not that this picture makes it look very good." She slapped her menu shut.

The photo of a hamburger caught his attention; patty shimmering with fats, dripping with cheese, a color not found in nature, bun clearly dry and stale. Really, the last thing he wanted to do was eat.

"*Shit.*" She'd been looking around the restaurant, but now she was staring straight at him. "Shit," she repeated. "Oh, shit. Your work…your paintings. Oh, shit."

The waitress had unexpectedly arrived, pad out, pencil ready. "So-what-will-ya-have?" she asked, looking out the window at the gleaming glass and flashing headlights outside, not at them.

"Shit," Shelly stammered, face bleached. One purple-nailed hand drummed on the tabletop.

"Give us a few more minutes," he said. "Please."

The waitress rolled her eyes. "Sure thing," she snapped, marching off.

Reaching across the table, he wrapped a tan hand around her quickly drumming right. With the contact, the tapping stopped and she focused.

"Shelly—" he said, controlled and precise.

"Fuck," she said, the tension easing out of her hand, her fingers, her shoulders. A smile crinkled her cheeks as he relaxed his grip, pulled back his hand. The signal was apparent, a warm light on the sudden chilly darkness at their table. Even though she didn't need to say it, she did anyway: "I'm okay."

Feeling he had to say something, anything, he stupidly echoed her. "Okay…" Guilty, he wanted her to be okay, all right, safe and happy, but he also wanted her gone, removed, cut away. Everything would be so simple without her.

Grinning weakly, she scanned for the waitress. "If it's not too much trouble, can we have a Denver omelet, coffee and—whattayouwant, babe?"

"Oh…um, a hamburger. That's all."

"—and a hamburger. Rare, right? Just show the cow a picture of the stove."

After a long minute, Shelly spoke. "I forgot about your paintings. I told myself they were just some Goth claptrap, you know? Twisted stuff just for the sake of being twisted, a nice little hook to hang up for publicity. 'Come see the freak who paints in blood!' Maybe goat, maybe cow, maybe 'something else.' Ohhhhhh…" Waving hands over the table, she did the ghost voice. "But they weren't cow or goat, were they? Why the fuck did you do them, Doud?"

"To thank them," he said. His chest was tight. "It made me feel better."

"But you stopped." Pausing, she seemed to rifle through her emotions, trying to figure out how she felt. "So how many portraits have you painted since 1910, Doud? Lots? A few?"

"1850," he said. "I was born in New York, in 1850."

Obviously strained, without a doubt wound too tight, at least it didn't look like she was getting ready to run. "Paintings. Tell me how many paintings. I don't know what number will freak me out, but you have to at least give me a number. Maybe a few means you had no choice, maybe a lot means... Shit, I don't know what it means. You say you have to, you don't have a choice, right? You try and make it up to them by painting their portraits. That's something, I guess."

"I hope it is...was," he said. The past tense made him rigid. Was, as in *no more*. It was a stupid thing, really; putting brush to canvas, using their medium as his message, as a way of giving them (if only by proxy) a kind of immortality. He only started hanging them on gallery walls ten years ago. Ridiculous, but it had helped make his day by day, by day by day life tolerable. He told himself that hanging someplace, having people see them, would make his subjects live on longer than just painting them in private. Much better than just painting and then destroying them as he used to do. Monsters didn't paint pictures of their victims, or display them. He did.

No, he used to.

He found himself talking, not really paying much attention to what he was saying: "Not a lot, but too many. When I was young I killed by accident..." and there, then, right in front of him was that boy from the docks. The one his father had caught him with. But then it had only been sex, two naked boys behind a store. After his father had loosened Doud's teeth and told him never to come home again, the boy had tracked Doud down to the old theatre he'd been living under. In that basement, they'd kissed, the boy sad at causing him such misfortune. A pair of lips offered in consolation. Dust, mildew, rot, the two of them cuddling in the darkness, amid faded sequins and tattered lace.

"I've learned to control it," he repeated, trying to rid himself of the remembrance, but it hung around his neck with tiny, sharp nails: the roar of the audience above, the smell of greasepaint from the actors, the wheezing breaths of the boy. Pale blue eyes. Freckles. His name. He should at least remember the boy's name. His first kiss. But as they'd kissed it'd changed, from loving into something else.

The boy was also the first person Doud had killed. "I don't do it because I want to, only when I have to. About every six months. Sometimes longer, sometimes shorter. I try to be careful. I can't help myself. It's the way I am."

"What are you?"

"I don't know. I've never met anyone else like me. Never even heard of anything like me. I was born this way. A freak."

He'd said this before, of course; back in his apartment, and as they rode in the car shortly afterwards, but this time she was really watching, listening. Her attention was like a too-bright light. He blinked. "It hurts," he whispered. "Painting helped me cope, but the pain never goes completely away."

"It's about apologizing, right? The paintings, I mean," she said. " 'It's the thought that counts,' my mother would say. Okay, like I wish she'd say, if she'd ever haul her ass out of a bottle long enough to do anything but belch. But like I wanted dear old mom to say, at least you feel sorry. That's why, right?"

"Yes. But I can't do it anymore."

Then the waitress was standing by their table, carrying platters of food.

Her arrival was a good distraction. Shelly provided most of what little conversation they had after, slipping into their usual dinner banter of flamboyantly describing the meal, rarely positive and mostly negative. "I didn't believe it was possible. Have you ever seen, in your life, a bad omelet?"

The hamburger wasn't even mediocre, but he ate it anyway, trying to push back even the remotest hint of emptiness, eating to fill, stuff, any available space.

Their plates emptied too quickly; the occupation of their time exhausted, leaving nothing but streaks of catsup, wilted lettuce, granules of salt, a few shreds of egg, a sad slice of tomato, and lots and lots of yellow, glistening grease.

Even though the waitress hadn't brought the check, he dug for his wallet. He knew, and suspected Shelly concurred, that the day had gone on far too long. He put down way too much. They would forget the waitress, but the waitress would never forget them. "Ready?"

"Honey, I was born ready," she said, a favorite joke, as she climbed out of the seat.

Outside, the night was sharp and clear. Whatever corner of the city they were in, there wasn't enough blazing advertising to completely obscure the stars.

"Pretty," she said, standing close to him, her arm snaking around his. "I don't look up enough, you know? Take them for granted, I guess. Damned pretty stars."

"They are," he said, uncomfortable. "I'm getting tired."

"We should get to the motel. Inspect our accommodations. Do you think they'll have mints on our pillows?"

"Doubt it. It looks like only a two star Roach Motel." The humor was stiff, like moving a limb that had fallen asleep.

"I've always wondered if Roach Motels have wake-up calls, or tiny Gideon Bibles. Ever wonder what the roach bible would be like? Go forth and multiply, and multiply, multiply, and multiply—"

The car seemed too far away, she was wrapped too tightly around his arm. "Can't say I've wondered about that, Shelly."

"That's my problem: I think too much about this kind of shit. Like that waitress. I can't help but think that she must have been happy once. Just simple odds. No one can be miserable all their lives, can they?"

The car. Finally. "Probably not," he said, knowing different.

In synch they climbed in. Key in the ignition, turn, the engine catching the first time, a smooth mechanical purr, barely audible. Fine machinery working perfectly was very satisfying. Comfortable. No matter what happened, his car would always start.

They drove the short distance to the motel. She took a stab at talking a few times, but Doud didn't respond, pretending to be absorbed in driving.

The motel may have been a chain, but this one was obviously a weak link. The usual things people depended on were there but scuffed, broken, stained, or warped out of shape. Even the signifying number in the huge plastic sign was burnt out, making it simply MOTEL.

Despite its corrosion and decay, it was surprisingly busy. Vans pulling trailers, a semi-trailer, station wagons, a few dust-fogged luxury cars. He hoped it would be quiet that night, but was already preparing himself to listen to some insomniac channel surfing in the next room.

Getting out, not quite as together as when they'd entered, they walked towards their adjoining rooms. Hers first: 13. His next door: 14.

"Doud," she whispered.

"Yes?"

"You said you've been this way all your life, right?" Her eyes were wide and brown even in the hard yellow sodium parking lot lights. Nearby, a soda machine's refrigerator switched on with a vibrating, ponderous hum.

Even through the heavy sound and his own fluttering anxiety, there was a quality to her way of speaking he'd never heard before. A softness, a suppleness of tone and phrase, pliant and warm. Inviting. "That's right," he said with a strength he didn't feel. "All my life."

"I see." Twisting the knob, she gave the door to her room a hefty push. "Oh, one more thing."

"Yes, Shelly?"

"I don't want you to think, you know, that I might run out on you tonight and leave you behind. Like I said, this has all been, well, kind of a bit much, but you're my friend, maybe my only good friend, and I really don't understand what the hell's going on right now, but I'm here for you. Okay?"

"Thank you." He hunted for anything better, but all that came out was "Sleep well."

The grin was warm, sweet and sincere, and then gone as she went into her room. The door closed with the soft sigh of wood sliding across old carpeting.

In his own room, he stretched out on the bed and stared at the cracks in the ceiling for hours, unable to sleep.

Just before he fell asleep, he wished, honestly, sincerely, that she would run off during the night. Just quietly vanish. The fantasy was warm and comforting; the hush of her door opening, padding stocking feet across the parking lot, out to the main road. Then? Then she'd wave, bouncing up and down, until a car stopped. She'd laugh, make up some story for the truck driver, delivery man, suburban family, pimpled teenager out for a late drive, talking them into taking her to a bus station, or a rental car place open for some reason, at that late hour. Safe, then, away, distant, but most importantly, *gone.*

Sleep tugged, wrapping him in gentle warmth, mind beginning to drift. *Go away. Before something happens to you. Before Sergio…or I…happen to you*, he thought just before sinking, dropping off to sleep.

CHAPTER 7

Flocked wallpaper. After a blink: still flocked wallpaper. He might as well be in any one of a thousand other, similar, hotel rooms he'd slept in over the years. Is that's what going to happen? An endless avalanche of broken associations, and hazy recollections? A cerulean sky bringing hope, tied always to a gap in the clouds over gray-roofed New York? The scent of vanilla making him shake in fear, connected to the blinding, flashing pain of Papa's hand descending on him in the bakery?

Dream lethargy sung a siren tune, trying to pull him back to bed. He rubbed his eyes to keep from looking at the wallpaper again and sat up.

The sheets felt like starched tissue paper. He hated motel beds, especially cheap places. Climbing out, he sat on the edge of the mattress and scratched himself. *Sergio.* Name, face, body, personality tumbled through his mind. He couldn't recall what he'd exactly been dreaming about, or whether he'd even been dreaming at all. Another cause and effect memory? Old boyfriend conjured from a bedspread, the musk of mildewed carpeting, morning light through a dirty window? The room, though, didn't bring any more of his ex-lover to mind. It was just a motel room, a gloomy space used for a few hours by sad people.

What am I going to do? He realized he didn't have any idea, at least not in the long term. Short term, though, was accessible:

Get to Barstow. Hole up. Think. Figure out what to do. Eventually get back to the city, try and find him. And then?

The knock shocked him, like cold water in the face. "Y-yes? Who is it? What do you want?" he sputtered, a machine-gun stammer.

"Rise and shine, sleepyhead. Unless you want to spend another fabulous night in these palatial accommodations."

"Um—just give me a minute. I'll be right out." Shower? But for some reason he didn't want to. He hadn't packed, so he didn't even have as much as a toothbrush. Unpeeling crackling plastic from a cheap tumbler, he filled it from the spitting, hissing, faucet. A few swishes around his mouth, then out into the sink.

Then underwear, t-shirt, shirt, socks, pants, shoes, all done up with zipper, buttons, loops, buckle, then straightened to satisfaction. Sergio, though, stayed with him, his face lurking nearby, his voice too close. His slippery, melodic accent that defied Americanization, seemed to tickle, live and fresh, in his ear as Doud scanned the room for anything forgotten.

Doud used to worry about Sergio's cough. Plaster, gypsum, sawdust, paint fumes, turpentine, kerosene. There were always too many wicked, powdery things in his studio. A cough one day could too easily turn into a cough with blood the next.

Blood and handkerchiefs. *No, not now*, but he still couldn't help but remember their walk on Hollywood Boulevard. Mr. Griffith's *Intolerance* was in the can, the money in their pockets. New suits for the two of them. Doud and Sergio, a pair of Dapper Dans out strolling that city of dreams, lost in their own.

Then bird shit on Doud's sleeve. "Let me get that," Sergio'd said, offering a square of lace. It took Doud only an instant to see, then realize, that there was blood on the handkerchief. Too much blood for even emphysema.

Blood red on white fabric, clear and irrefutable evidence that Sergio wasn't his lover. Sergio had turned beast.

It was then that Doud knew he'd have to kill him.

Stay in the present. Focus, he thought, fighting the memory.

He won that battle, at least, his prize being the understanding not every recollection would end up haunting him, just the special ones. The memories that, no matter how far he went, or how long he lived, would always remain as close as the next accidental reminder. Monsters lurking behind every yard of flocked wallpaper.

"There you are, darlin'. Thought for a second there you'd decided to retire to this cultural Mecca. Ready to go?" Shelly said when he finally stepped out.

"Let's put this behind us," he said with a false humor he didn't feel, closing the door behind him.

CHAPTER 8

ThEY WERE BACK ON the freeway, silence again between them. Shelly's body was tight and tense, obviously ready, willing, and eager to talk, but clearly not knowing how to start.

The day was remarkably picturesque. The sun hung behind streaks of thin clouds, transforming them into golden swatches across the sky. Below them, California was done in earth shades, a baked terra cotta landscape. Doud, always the artist, lost himself in the composition and colors of the view. Besides, it was better than thinking about Shelly, Sergio, or the rest of his long, wet, and bloody life.

After long miles and minutes, Shelly clearly reached her limit and finally sputtered out: "Doud? Come on, hon, talk to me. This is driving me nuts. It isn't every day you find out that one of your best friends is…well, shit, you got to admit this is all pretty weird. Tell something, anything. Tell me about Sergio. Why are you so scared of him?"

It really wasn't something he wanted to talk about, but a sharp stab of guilt reminded him that he was responsible for her. He owed her at least to answer as many of her questions as he could. "He was…a lover, but then he became a monster," he said, not taking his eyes from the road.

"I've had some boyfriends like that. Tell me why."

"I wanted to be with someone like me. I prayed that Sergio was going to be the one. I was wrong."

"So he's like you? But you said you're the only one. Did you make him? Shit. I didn't know you could do that. You can do that? To anyone?"

"I can. I haven't done it often, but, yes, I can. Sometimes I get so lonely, I just want someone to share my life with, someone who'll understand. I've always had to…undo it, though. Fix my mistakes." A new hush stretched between, he just driving the car. Then: "I… do what I have to do to live. I don't do it because I like it. Sergio didn't understand that. He liked it, the killing I mean, so I had to stop him. I thought I had, I mean, but I obviously didn't. Now he's back, so I'm running away."

"God. I didn't know that. I mean…to be able to do that. Make more of yourself, I mean." Without waiting for permission, her purse came open and she lit up. After a long, steady drag: "Do you think he can make more? Do you think he can do it, too, like you can?"

"I don't know. I don't think so."

She stared out at the road. "You wanted someone. Who the hell couldn't understand that? You're a good man, you deserve someone who cares about you."

"Shelly," he said, putting his foot down, quickly pushing the car up to, then over, the speed limit. "I kill people." A truck passed on the right, kicked dust and hot wind into the car. "I've tried…I've tried to stop myself. I can't. I'm a monster, too."

No, don't think about that. Don't think about that rooming house in New York, don't think about 1901. Don't think about the razor, brand new one from that little shop on 51st Street. Don't think about the big bottle of brandy. Don't think about my wrist reflecting in the blade's shine.

Don't think, but he did: torturing himself with memory. Blood in a tin bucket, the room rolling like the deck of a ship. Then the hunger roaring in his ears.

Joshua, that was his name. He lived down the hall. He had liked gin, played the mouth harp, and went down to the docks to watch the great ships steam into the harbor. Too much blood having trickled into the bucket from his attempted suicide, Doud's body had acted on its own, had demanded filling.

Joshua had simply been available.

After his body had taken what it had needed, reducing Joshua to nothing but dust and crumbling bones in his arms, Doud had returned to consciousness. Aware again, Doud had screamed, had roared in pain, when he realized that the man now sloshing in his belly had been a sweet soul, a man of easy laughter, a smile whenever they'd passed each other in the rooming house. He hadn't deserved to die.

"That's bullshit. Let me finish." This to a quick turn of his head, his mouth opening to speak. "Okay, I may not have known you for years and years and all, and sure as hell not for hundreds, but I still think enough to know what kind of guy you are. You're a good man, Doud. Maybe that's why I haven't run away." The last softer, lighter, more to herself than to him.

Don't think, but he did. The roofer, how he'd baited him with beer, come on to him in the alley. *Kiss me*, Doud had asked, wishing for that simplest of affections. But at the same time hoping that the burly man would instead raise his fists, start swinging, and give Doud a reason to kill him. Doud had been lonely, but he'd also been hungry, had needed to feed.

Sideward glance to Shelly, fury cramping in his bubbling belly, churning up the roofer's stolen life. *A good man? No, I'm not good.*

And I'm certainly not a man.

Opening his mouth, skin stretching, throat contracting. Never satiated, never asleep, never full, never happy, never gratified, never content, never satisfied, the pit in his belly, his awful hunger, woke up. It demanded feeding.

This is what I am.

He wanted Shelly to scream like they all had, before Doud had kissed them, had sucked them dry. All he had to do was let it loose, give it permission to suck the liquid life from her. He wanted to show her what he really was. He wanted to prove to her that he was a monster.

But he couldn't do it.

His throat contracting, lips shrinking, tightening, he swallowed his hunger, locked it away in his belly. Denied, it slunk back down, his muscles aching from being tensed but then denied action.

"Sleepy?" she asked, mistaking his gaping mouth for a yawn. "Should have stopped for coffee, I guess."

CHAPTER 9

S HELLY HADN'T BEEN TO Barstow in years, and being driven through the town, she remembered why. Dust devils competed with 4x4s on brand new, soulless roads. It was a place of chain stores, fast food joints, and mini-malls, each with a slight rustic flair so the natives could be proud of the past they'd paved over. *Probably poured it right over the flattened coyotes and tumbleweeds.*

For someone who hadn't been in town for, well, a very long time, Doud certainly drove like he knew where he was going. Cruising through downtown after sliding off the freeway, they worked their way out to even dustier back streets. Even though Shelly had questions piling up in her mind, she didn't say anything. Doud's nervousness was palpable, solid. His knuckles were tight on the wheel.

The town vanished bit by bit, replaced by low, rolling hills covered by dead, yellow grass, stitched together like sections of quilt by sagging, rusted chain link fences. Occasionally they'd pass a cinderblock and plywood building—a bar, feed, or auto parts store —but otherwise the road was deserted. The questions cramped her stomach, but she stayed quiet, just watching the road go by. A billboard: I CARE, SIGNED GOD. Another question was added to the ache: Was he proof of something, or proof of the absence of something? Did this mean that some myths were real, or that Doud was completely new? The outskirts of Barstow were hot and dull, the people shuffling through the heat, proudly wearing their mediocrity. Another question: *What else have I been missing?*

"We're here," he said, turning the wheel sharply. She twisted her view from the side window as well, looking forward.

Off on a dusty, pothole-mined side road, a few hundred or so feet from the paving, the house was simple, just two stories. Three windows on top just below a gently peaked roof with two modest dormers, and a stubby brick chimney. Two windows below, between them a thick oak door without a knocker. If it had ever had a color, it was long gone, harshly scrubbed, bleached, and cracked from years of incessant sunlight. For old architecture, it was free of ornamentation, the slightest taste of gingerbread. It didn't have character, or even any sense of being a 'home' for anything, except some tree rats and raccoons.

As they'd pulled into town, he had mentioned that he paid a person regularly to give it light maintenance. Although it was stark, she realized it wasn't completely lifeless; just lean on life. The dead weeds on either side kept back by a leaning wooden fence were cut short. The front yard, what there was of it, was also close-cropped. The windows were all intact, the interior hidden by thick, faded Army-green curtains.

The house was alone, on the side of a low hill. Beyond it, Shelly could see the pale geometry of the freeway, the darker streaks of Barstow's surface streets, and the dull rectangles of buildings and houses. Between there and here was what seemed to be an endless field of even more weeds, wild, tall and brown in steadily descending death down the sloping hillside.

Doud parked with the Lexus's nose pointing toward the front door. "Well," he said with a slight grin. "This is it." He seemed embarrassed; as if he was worried their final destination might not have been worth the trip.

The house was old, and so, supposedly, was he. There was ample room for laughing, but she didn't quite do that. But since she was still Shelly, she had to at least smile and say, "Let's go in. I'm curious to see what you've done to the old place."

Outside, morning air was warm, dry, threatening to be a hot afternoon. The sky was piercing blue, an oppressive aqua. She began to dig through her purse for her sunglasses, an unconscious LA thing, but then stopped when she realized they would be inside in just a few seconds. Embarrassed, she snapped the bag shut, slipped it over her shoulder, and trotted to catch up to Doud, who was already climbing the creaky wooden steps.

"The lock should be okay," he said, on the porch, ring of keys in one hand. "It's one of the things I have them check."

Steps groaning in accompaniment, she was next to him in a moment. He was talking out of discomfort, she realized. *What must it be like? Back here after all this time? With me? With psycho ex-boyfriend somewhere out there?*

Am I really believing this?

Finding the right key, he slipped it into the brass keyhole, gave it a turn, and shouldered the door open. Cool, stale air blew in, carrying the faintly sour smell of dust and mildew. A flight of stairs headed up to the second floor, a faded burgundy runner of carpet held down by tarnished brass rods, all revealed by light coming from a window at the top, framing blue sky and the corner of a cloud. Leading the way, he headed toward the living room. Turning to close the door behind her, she noticed that his heavy, drumming steps had stopped.

"Who are you? What are you doing here?" It was Doud's voice from the living room, bass and thunderous.

Pulse fluttering in her neck, she spun to look. He was in a dim, sparse room, faded rug on the floor, the only furniture a huge old sofa tightly wrapped in clouded sheets of plastic. Overhead, an ornate frosted glass fixture, unlit. On one wall, a square marked where a painting had hung for a long time, now gone. In the middle of the room, facing the dining room, was Doud. His body was rigid, stiff, his hands tight fists at his side.

Standing in the doorway toward the back of the house was another man. Not Sergio, she realized with some relief, feeling her body slacken, but mind still racing. *Homeless creep, bum who'd found a safe place to sleep.* No time to *really* get a good look. Just barely enough time to see torn jeans, no shirt, no shoes, dirty streaks across a young, surprisingly well-defined chest, scraggly beard, knotted, filthy hair that could have been brown, but was probably just unwashed.

They faced each other, the young man panting like a dog that'd been out running. Heavy, heaving breaths. "Get out," Doud rumbled, stepping toward him. But then he stopped, as if hit by something only he could see, only he was aware of.

The man spoke, lips moving ponderously, but he was too far away. She couldn't make out what he said.

No words, but she *did* hear a low moan, an inhaling tone that carried easily across the room, growing quickly in intensity. The man's mouth was stretching with the suctioning tone. It was a large sound, a hungry sound, and it needed a larger hole, so the man opened and opened and opened, more and more and more, to give it room.

Lips stretching, jaw hinging wide, he inhaled. She pictured the corners of his mouth tearing, ripping like soggy cardboard, blood pouring down his neck, dripping thick, heavy drops on his shoulders, sheeting his chest in red, flowing around the dark spots of his nipples, from the stretching. But that was her mind, what she expected.

It wasn't what happened.

Instead, the hole of his mouth gaped wider and wider, revealing the wet pit of his ragged mouth, showing a cavernous interior of irregular teeth, and shadowed pockets where others had fallen out. As his mouth expanded, he howled even more, an inexhaustible appetite's bellowing roar, a storm of need that rose into a hurricane.

Through it all, Doud stood, braced against the sucking wind, arms locked to his sides, dusty air rushing past him and into the stranger's bottomless maw.

Then, in one moment to the next, he wasn't there. He wasn't standing, facing that hideous, funneling draw, but instead had vanished, gone with a clap of thunder louder than her cries, even louder than the blaring suction from the stranger's mouth.

Later, she'd be able to string it all together, to figure out what had happened. But that was later. For her right then it was all just a series of events in hot, quick, seconds of time.

Doud disappeared, transforming into a blur that began where he'd been standing, rushed toward the stranger. Then the stranger vanished as well, their sonic booms combining into a single blast that shook the house's rafters, sending rivulets of dust from between ceiling beams, sneezed up from between floor boards.

Their blurred outlines spun around each other, tornadoes of half-seen, barely-glimpsed men: what could possibly have been arms, what maybe were legs, what might be fists, all through a haze of grit and acceleration. Then the twister of their battle canted, swung and bolted out of the room, and back towards the kitchen.

Shelly ran after them, her heart an angry fist in her chest, and her breath like a hot rasp in her throat. Didn't know why, didn't stop to think, didn't deal with the insanity of it, she just ran from the living room to the kitchen.

A window was gone, smashed out of the wall; frame and glass, plaster and lath torn, broken and ripped away. Clouds of gypsum swirled in the air. The house complained of the loss in moaning creeks, a sound she could barely hear over the screaming winds. Still thoughtless, she ran to the hole, cautiously peering out: a short drop to still more yellowed grass, a sea of dead weeds, the city far beyond. But below her, below the destroyed wall, was a dust devil, a twister of too-fast-to-believe movements.

Within the tornado was a shadow play, their almost-forms and half-seen figures still battling. In accompaniment were dual roars of fury, explosive percussions of fists.

Then it was over. The winds eased, fading to lazy swirls of lethargic dirt. In the center of it all, no longer almost, half-seen, clouded, blurred, was a man.

He looked up at her.

And Shelly remembered her mother.

One night, when her mother was very, very drunk, she'd pulled a book from their lone bookcase, a thick book stolen from a school or library. Cracking it open, she'd shown to a twelve-year-old Shelly. "This is what people will do to you," she said in a gin-drenched tone, showing a plate of photos. Years later, Shelly would put a name and a location to the photograph: *Dachau*.

The man standing below her, in a circle of torn and blasted weeds, had a Dachau face, sunken, caved in, desiccated. Eyes like glistening blisters locked with hers. He was drained, vacant. He was an empty man, barely a shell.

In those gleaming eyes, a hundred or so feet away from her, she saw an unmistakable thing: *hunger*.

Then his mouth…opened: wider and wider, more and more, gaping, yawning, until there was nothing but a great maw, a pit to an eternal, infernal appetite.

A pause. A moment. A second. A new quality in those boiled-egg eyes, that callow and sunken face, easily read from even so far away and through the dust-heavy morning. *Recognition.* He knew her. Tearing his gaze away from hers, he bolted, sprinting through the weeds. Too quick, inhumanly fast, he was a dirt trail through the wild field, away from the house, away from the town, up and over the hills, faster than even her eyes could track.

Gone. A cloud of dark yellow dirt and broken stalks were all that remained.

Shelly, frozen dead still, looked towards where he'd gone. Shelly, with a single thought ringing too distinctly, too loudly in her mind.

That was Doud.

CHAPTER 10

Doud, standing in his old living room, and saying "Get out," had instantly known two things. One: the man was a stranger; he'd never seen him before in his life. Two: the man was a stranger only in appearance. Doud instantly recognized him for *what* he was.

Mumbling gravelly words only Doud could hear, the creature had given him a message. And with the message, even more information: who had transformed him. Who'd made him.

Seeing, understanding, knowing all this, Doud felt a spike of hot rage. It felt good: a pure, justified emotion.

The *thing* in front of him was nothing but bottomless hunger. It was what he'd fought all his life against: both in accidentally creating, or becoming himself. Doud instantly wanted to kill it.

Its mouth opened. Standing firm, tensed against the suction beginning to pull at him from the gaping maw, Doud thought, clear, quick and certain: *It's a trap. Left here to deliver a message, to kill me if possible.*

Possible? Probable…the monster was more than hungry, it was closer to ravenous, and Doud's fury was immediately replaced by dread. Distorted by starvation, the monster had no will, no mind, beyond delivering its simple message. It was nothing but a hideous vacuum, a primordial need to pull in anything living within reach.

There wasn't time to do anything but act. He knew the cost was high and dangerous, but the monster was too damned close. Doud was well within grabbing range, and once grabbed, its mouth would clamp over his, and it would then utterly consume Doud's warm and wet life.

No choice. Doud accelerated.

The world slowed, the air grew hot and thick. In front of him, the monster and its suction eased, Doud now moving too fast to feel its full effect. Lurking at the limits of his peripheral vision, the familiar red glow began, the twisting of his visual spectrum. The floor was slippery, traction harder and harder to maintain as he stepped forward.

He couldn't stop if he wanted to, momentum dictating his actions as much as his will. The monster, moving at a diminished rate, appeared frozen and unknowing, mouth gaping in hunger. Crouching down, Doud stepped forward, aiming for the monster's center, pointing his elbow at its chest, specifically its sternum.

The monster's eyes began glazed, unfocused, unable to see him for his new speed, but as Doud headed across the living room, its eyes became clearer. It began to understand what was happening. That was very bad news, and Doud felt drumming fear in his chest again. If he'd been able to travel fast enough, to surprise it, then he'd have had an advantage, but with each step the monster was becoming more and more aware of him, beginning to match Doud's accelerated pace.

Doud could see its face now, stretched by its ravenous mouth. Harsh, filthy, dotted with pimples and blackheads, here was a person on intimate terms with want: an ideal device to be made into Sergio's murder weapon. Even frightened, panicked, and desperate, Doud felt a raw flow of clear mind. *Bastard*. He'd never hated Sergio more.

They collided. If their speeds hadn't been nearly matched, if the monster hadn't started to accelerate as well, Doud would have passed right through it, a flesh and bone missile, skeleton and muscle bullet. But the monster had tapped into its own negligible reserves, had started to burn whatever bloody fuel it had left. Moving at nearly the same speed now, they were twin blurs of speed, too fast for anyone else to see.

Not quite fast enough, though: Doud still took it by surprise, just not fatally. Impetus in his favor, he crashed into the monster, pushing it back across the dusty floor, both now traveling too fast, with not enough traction to stop. Hands burnt and blistered from air friction, he fumbling for any kind of leverage, trying to turn it towards the rapidly approaching kitchen wall.

Sliding along with him, the monster's face was tilted down towards him, mouth even wider than before. Even moving too quickly for anyone else to see, Doud still felt its suction, and knew he was inches from a battle he didn't want to fight, couldn't win. He may have the experience but the monster had raw, primal hunger—and desperation.

With the creature's back twisted towards it, Doud shielding himself behind, they hit the wall. At his heightened perception, his extreme speed, the wall bent, depressing deeper and deeper until it finally cracked and broke, shock waves rippling away from their point of impact, undulating across its surface.

He'd done this before, but never this long, and never this fast. Lurking in the back of his mind was the knowledge of the cost he'd have to pay when it was all over, but Doud pushed it all aside, he couldn't let himself become distracted. He was too close to that horrible mouth.

They fell in stretched time, Doud struggling with the fanatically determined monster, trying to keep its hideous suction away, hoping that hitting ground would do what hitting the wall hadn't. In those seconds like minutes, Doud's muscles went from aching in pain to shrieking in agony. He was burning up. He was running dry. Whatever reserves he'd had, whatever had been left of the roofer in his belly, were gone.

His body fought him to act on its own, the inexhaustible hunger demanding control.

He had to hurry. Soon, too soon, he wouldn't be Doud anymore. In another few moments he'd become only a need, just a mouth, pure hunger without reason. He'd become a monster. Another ravenous monster.

Luck—or just enough consciousness—stayed with him. Twisting and turning as they dropped through the thick, hot air, he barely managed to keep himself positioned on top. Then they weren't falling, but instead hitting the ground, the slow impact, a ponderous shove up and through the body of the creature, and into Doud's hands and arms. Doud's inertia did what his elbow couldn't, crushing the monster into the backyard dirt.

Rebounding from the surface, still in fast time, a tickle of awareness remained in Doud's mind as he ripped his charred hands across the monster's chest, dried skin tearing like rotted cloth between his fingers: *Burning up.*

Slackened for a moment when they hit the ground, the monster's mouth suddenly yawned larger. Panic flashed through Doud's brain as he pummeled its chest, desperate to escape its sucking maw. Ablaze with speed, he missed, hitting earth instead. Fists hitting soft soil like a bullet fired at a sandbag, there remained just enough resistance to shove Doud back, away from the monster's screaming mouth.

His hand, though, broke, the dried tissues tearing, the desiccated bones snapping. Normally he wouldn't have felt it, could have even accelerated.

But there wasn't any Doud left to feel.

Liquid reserves gone, all of it finally sucked dry, all that remained of Doud was a mouth, a ravenous hole. As a thinking person, a being with choice, Doud was gone.

Only the hunger remained.

Later, he'd think about that morning, and hope that he won because he wanted to win, that he had something inside himself that gave him an edge, a touch more humanity that made him more than just a mouth that drank, a body that ate, and a never-abiding need. He hoped, but like everything else in his life, including what he was and how he came to be, it was a question he'd never be able to answer completely.

As he battered himself away from its mouth and the vacuum threatening to suck away what little moisture Doud's body had left, the monster ran completely dry.

Collapsing, imploding, crumbling, it consumed the last few ounces of its own liquid life. In its furious hunger, the monster had only one thing remaining to feed on: itself. With his one good hand, Doud's hunger grabbed the monster's neck, and stood up, hauling up whatever was left of the thing.

Swinging the monster's remains, skin of its neck ripping and tearing, muscles and tissues underneath deteriorating like dried, dead earth, Doud's raging emptiness brought its blackened and split mouth to its own crumbling lips, trying desperately to drink what little life remained.

But the monster was empty, gone, dead. Nothing was left.

The world acquired sound, the ground achieved traction, the air thinned, the rose red glow ceased. As his body slowed from the blinding acceleration Doud had forced on it, the monster's body completely disintegrated. A body once 95% water having become nothing but a desiccated 5%, falling apart into dust, ash, and a few brittle bones: life and moisture gone.

In a circle of dirt and flattened weeds, breathing heavily, hoarsely, Doud's desperate body crouched down, broken in too many places to stand upright.

Hunger. His body had used itself up in the fight, and now it needed food, and it needed it *now*. It didn't care who, didn't care how. It needed, and it wouldn't stop until it ate.

Lifting its head, the hunger saw life just above it, a figure framed by the smashed wall of the house above. The mouth, sensing nutrition, opened. Muscles obeying the hunger, the body tensed to move, to leap in pursuit.

But then it didn't. Emaciated, used up, drained, *Doud* stood in a flattened field of weeds and looked up.

Doud, not just his hunger, saw the woman looking out and down at him from of a gaping hole in the house.

Doud saw her. *Doud* knew her.

Doud knew what would happen if he stayed. His mind should not have been there, his hunger should have completely squeezed it out in its ferocious need to eat, but it was there nonetheless. No time to think about the *why*. No time to think about the *how*. No time to do anything but get the hell away from there. Doud had barely a few seconds before the hunger and its bellowing, deafening, demands, overruled his consciousness.

He ran, not as fast as he had before, but as fast as he could without burning up. Forcing his way through the dead stalks, he tried to get as far away as he could.

He ran, to get his body, and its howling, growling hunger away from the house.

Away from Shelly.

CHAPTER II

WHEN DOUD RETURNED TO being Doud, had completely regained his consciousness, he awoke holding the powdered remains of someone's life. The remains of a death, a new death, in his arms.

The second of the day. The monster, with its message, had been the first. Frank had been the second.

The name was on his driver's license, which Doud found in a fat leather wallet in his empty, dusty, coveralls: Frank A. McHenry. 46 years old. A few credit cards, an ATM card, a Blockbuster membership card, but the license was more than enough, because it gave Doud all he needed to be miserable. Frank McHenry. Once alive, now only a set of rough, workman's clothes, a few shreds of dried skin, a pile of dirt and dust, a pitiful nest of hair, and some fragments of broken, brittle bones. Not even a face remained to match against the photo on the license. Frank was dead, drained of fluid. Blood, pus, bile, saline…everything gone, sucked away.

By Doud.

Awareness had returned to Doud holding Frank's dusty residue in his arms. The knowledge of what he'd done becoming a crushing weight, pushing Doud down to his knees. With each movement, Frank's remains broke further, bones disintegrating more and more, until he was holding only empty coveralls, dust streaming with a low hiss out of the legs, pouring over the bib, rivulets around the straps.

Even though he didn't remember killing Frank, it didn't ease Doud's guilt. Even though he didn't have a single memory of the murder he knew what it must have been like. It must have started with a kiss.

Frank had probably been behind this tin shed, off the main road, a few hundred feet from Doud's house. He'd been taking a leak, something Frank probably did a lot back there. The narrow space between the shed and a yellowed hill reeked of stale urine and passed-through beer.

Then Doud had come on the scene. Maybe from around the side of the shed, or dropping down from the hill, or perhaps he'd been there already and Frank had walked around the corner and found him there, opportunity presenting itself.

Skeletal and wild, feral with need, ravenous, drained and desperate, Doud's hunger had met Frank McHenry—and kissed him.

I'm sorry, he said to the crumbling bones, the disintegrating hair, the powdery tissue. *I'm so sorry.* Again and again, rocking back and forth: *I'm so sorry. I'm so sorry. I'm so sorry.* Guilt was a fist in his gut, punching again and again.

No delusion, no hyperbole. Cold, simple fact: he'd killed, consumed him. This wasn't the roofer, someone he'd picked out, chosen. Frank's only crime had been innocently pissing in the dirt. *I'm so sorry.*

In the depths of his belly, bubbling, sloshing, Doud felt what was left of him. Liquid. Lively. The 95% fluidity of him, distilled, drawn out, swallowed, and used. Flexing his fingers, he tested his hand: bones reknit, repaired, muscles restored, skin tight and smooth. As good as new.

What was worse, he couldn't thank Frank for any of it, at least not how he used to. That avenue of forgiveness was long gone. No more portraits, never again. Another body blow, and more pain. He wanted to paint, desperately wanted to do what made him feel better. The itch was an ache, the ache was a cramp, the cramp was agony. It had worked, for him at least; a way of begging forgiveness for what he'd stolen, a bit of immortality for the victims as well. But those days were over.

For selfish reasons, which made it worse. It was over because someone, somewhere, had found a way to test blood, the substance of a person, and identify it perfectly. He didn't know how, but they could. The science was a mystery, but the idea was obvious: blood wasn't just blood anymore. He couldn't paint anymore, couldn't even paint then destroy it, let alone hang it up in a gallery somewhere, to have people think it was perhaps cow, maybe goat. Blood had become incriminating, perfect evidence, even the smallest unburned fleck of it. It identified, just like fingerprints.

I'm sorry, he thought, eyes cast down at the empty clothes, the swirling dust, white bits of bone, tumbling knots of hair. The remains of Frank. *I'm sorry.*

Then he remembered why he was there, in Barstow. He remembered Sergio.

Sitting on the feet of plaster elephants, gazing out at eternity. Talking about their long future together. Holding hands on Hollywood Boulevard. The one he thought he'd been waiting his whole, long life for. The one who seemed to be different, the one who wanted to be with Doud, and not just to become something other than human.

Then Doud had seen blood on that handkerchief and thought about an assistant director who couldn't be found, the same one Sergio had recently fought with. It was an easy, if painful formula, to put together. Blood on Sergio's handkerchief and a missing man.

Standing up, Doud automatically brushed Frank's dust from his own scorched and filthy clothes. With his rebuilt skin, blisters and scars gone, he didn't feel like a monster. Body repaired, his mind was the only thing that hurt.

Through the pain, he remembered Shelly's questions. What was he? He didn't have any answers: he'd no idea what he was. Myth? Fable? Children's story? Freak? Nothing came close. Sunlight was bright and warming, crosses just a symbol, and fire burned.

With Frank bubbling in his belly, he knew he wasn't human. But he knew one thing that made him more than just a mouth, or rampaging hunger. Guilt. He felt guilt, and shame. He felt sorry for Frank McHenry, and wished he hadn't had to die. Human shame, human guilt.

And human anger. Human fury. Frank was dead only because Sergio wanted to give Doud a message.

Doud felt. Mostly it was pain, but at least Doud felt. He might not have his portraits anymore, but he'd keep trying. Somehow, he'd find some way to apologize to people like Frank.

But he'd never apologize to Sergio. There was nothing remotely human about his ex-lover. Just joyous murder, a smiling kiss, and the pleasure in swallowing lives.

Doud might not be human, but Sergio was utterly inhuman.

CHAPTER 12

N O WAY COULD SHE stay in the house, not after seeing Doud look at her that way. Flinging the front door wide, she'd raced down the short steps. A thought litany of *oh god oh god oh god*, then, before it sank in that no one was behind her: *Got to get the fuck away from here.*

At the car, her panic faded. Legs weak, puppet strings cut, she slid down the hot metal door of the Lexus, sprawled on the ground.

With her re-found ability to think, she tried to puzzle it out. Wanting to get the fuck away was obvious, but there was also the fact that she was miles from town, didn't have the car keys, and had no place to go even if she wasn't miles from Barstow, and had the car keys.

"Oh, fuck." She really wanted a cigarette, but then remembered her purse was gone. Probably left it back in the house.

Okay… It wasn't just a crazy story. She'd seen him, really seen him, emaciated, drawn, callow, empty, panting like an overheated dog. Then he'd looked at her with bottomless hunger, a pure, ravenous appetite, wanting her.

No, that was her terror talking. A Basil Rathbone voice. There'd been something else there, a part of him that wasn't just NEED in bold, block letters. In the end he'd won, running away, parting the weeds, vanishing into the distance.

It was real, he'd been telling the truth. He was something else, about as something else as you could get. That terrified her, more than anything ever had. A something else that'd moved faster than she could see, howling like a hungry hurricane.

He was a something else that should have frozen her solid, making her scream and scream in terror until she couldn't any more. So why wasn't she? What was going on?

Rubbing the heels of her hands into her closed eyes, lights dancing in a personal darkness, she felt dirt grind against her lids. *I must look a sight. Wish I had my makeup.*

"Hey there. You okay?" A voice, rumbling through her black light show. Even before she opened her eyes, she knew the owner of it was standing only a few feet away. "You're looking kind of poorly, if you don't mind me saying."

Opening her eyes, she saw jeans ending in very used cowboy boots. Canting her head up, she added a T-shirt to the view, the rest backlit by the sun. Instantly, her face reddened, thinking of herself flopped out on the ground like that. Blinking against the bright light, she put out a hand for a lift up.

Climbing up, she dusted herself off. "I'm okay," she said, noticing that her nose was running. "Really, honestly, I'm okay. Just not having the best of days, you know. Thanks for asking."

"Problem with a boyfriend?" he said. His words were clipped and hesitant, suspicious. His eyes drifted past her towards the house. "If you don't mind me asking."

Couldn't blame him. "Not my boyfriend," she said, her own voice too sharp, the correction too firm. "A friend…anyway, it's nothing. Nothing real bad, anyway. I'll be okay."

Standing up, she got a much better view. He was tall and thin, hair short looking like it had been cut some months before, now growing out wildly. His face was tanned, like buffed leather. "No problem. Been there myself. Still, wouldn't be able to look at myself in the mirror if I didn't at least ask if you needed some help."

"Where's your suit of armor, Sir Galahad?" *Dummy. No reason to piss the guy off.* "Sorry, I'm, a bit rattled. Just got to get my head together."

"If it'll help, I'm willing to listen," he said, hooking his thumbs into the pockets of his jeans.

Where do I start? She felt like laughing, but bit it back. Drunk, dizzy flutters and thoughts clouded her mind, like the blood was struggling back from where her fear had shoved it. "Yeah, well…thanks. Actually, you could do me a favor. Could you give me a lift? I need to go to a motel. A place to take a shower, get my head together. I can pay for gas."

He showed off generous, very white teeth. "No problem. I can drop you on my way out to the highway." Suddenly uncomfortable: "You're more than welcome to tag along. Maybe bend my ear for a bit. I'm more than willing."

Grinning back at him, she reflected his white teeth with her beige ones. Mundane conversations, simple activities, in the middle of it all, making everything even stranger by comparison. Two days. Had it really been just two days? From trying to sell art to people with more money than taste, to… *Where am I? What's going on?* She shook her head. Galahad was a relief. Just a man. The first average, dull human being she'd spoken to since leaving LA. "Thanks for the offer, but I really just want to get cleaned up. Shit," she said, realizing. "I need to get my purse. Be right back."

"Sure thing. My truck's parked right over there. Take as long as you want."

"Thanks, I'll just be a sec."

Walking back towards the house, she noticed the door was still open. Venturing inside wasn't exactly high on her list of things she wanted to do right then, but she didn't have much a choice.

Glancing back over her shoulder, she saw him leaning back against a huge gray pickup, watching her. If she hopped in with him and rode off into the sunset, she could probably convince herself it had all been just a dumb daydream, a nasty nightmare. But if she walked in, she'd have to face reality.

Come on, get going, she thought, stepping inside the house.

The sun had started its drop, so the room wasn't exactly the same, shadows subtly changing it. Still, it was like going back in time. Just get in, get it, and get the fuck out.

The living room, dust swirling on the floor. In a corner, where it'd fallen, was her purse. Stepping across the floor, hearing her shoes scratch across the dirty wood, she caught the strap, pulled it close as she could, as fast as she could. The scratchy, embroidered material felt good, safe, familiar.

Out, out, out. She wanted to run, but held herself back, relishing the little act of bravery. Tight and tense, she strolled to the door, and out into the warm sunlight. One last thing: she shut the door behind her. *Take that.* But she had absolutely no idea to whom, or what, she directed the thought.

"Ready, darlin'?" Galahad said, still by the truck, showing off his fine parade of polished dentistry.

Shucky darn, yes. "Whenever you are." She said, rounding the machine and jumping up into the hot leather passenger seat. He joined her a second later. "Thanks again," she added, giving him a nice but hopefully uninviting smile.

"Any time," he said.

As the engine started, something made her say, "Wait a minute." Digging in her bag, she came up with a battered notebook, a fat chrome pen. "What's the name of a good motel downtown? One that wouldn't be full?"

"Around here, a room wouldn't exactly be a problem. Me, I'd suggest the Best Western. Cheap, clean rooms. Can't get better than that. I can drop you off right in front, if you'd like."

He'd transformed into a blur, moving too fast to be seen. He'd stood among yellow, dead weeds, his mouth grotesquely wide, starving for her. He'd wanted to kill her, drink her.

"Works for me." But she still wrote 'I'm at the downtown Best Western' on a page from the book, climbed out, went over to Doud's car, put it under a wiper blade.

"Note for your friend?" he said as she scrambled back in and slammed the door.

"Yeah, just don't want to disappear on him," she said.

"In my experience, some folks could do with some disappearing. But," he said, lifting fingers from the wheel, "that's not my place to say."

"It's not like that. Really."

"No problem, darlin'. Just some friendly advice is all." He shifted into gear and rolled down the dusty road.

Galahad's name was Vince. In town to check in on an old friend. He lived somewhere up north, near Death Valley, he added to his introduction. "A little place with a real pretty view of the end of the world." He was nice enough, and any other time Shelly may even have played with the idea of taking him out for drinks to see how high and fast he could rise on her jerk meter. But not today. Today all she wanted was for him to shut up and drive.

"Here we are," Vince said, truck rocking and yawing over a low curb. The motel was like every other Best Western she'd ever seen. No surprises. Thank god. She'd had enough of those to last a lifetime. "Sure not the best of accommodations, but it'll at least give you a nice place to put up your feet and drop your head."

"Thanks," she said, feeling for her wallet. Her rummaging took longer than it needed to, the smooth leather of her wallet slipping through her fingers several times. Drinks, food, chat: maybe it was just what she needed.

Seductive conformity, alluring normalcy: roll downhill. You know how to eat, Shelly, what a drink would taste like, how to laugh at his jokes, and you know what could happen after all that—if he isn't the total hick he appears to be.

"You know, talking can do a lot of good," he said, swiveling in his seat. "Now I don't know what's been going on with you. I'm not one to pry or anything, but I could just listen. You know, just to get it out."

"Yeah, right, thanks." Suddenly very tired, very dirty, back to that kind of ordinary would have to wait, at least until she had a hot shower. Good teeth or not, Vince would be driving home alone tonight.

My best friend's not human and we're both on the run from his ex-boyfriend, who wants to suck the life out of both of us. How's that for a start? "I appreciate it, honest to god, but to tell you the truth what I need right now is a damned hot shower and a really good night's rest. Thanks so much for the ride." She held out a folded ten.

"Nah, I can't take that. I'll just consider this my good deed for the day; giving a pretty lady a ride to town."

Must practice that grin in the mirror. Right back at him with her own less-than-perfect teeth, she put the money back, reached for a handle. "Well, Galahad, this is one very grateful lady. Thanks again."

Dropping out, moving to shut the door, he caught her attention one last time. "You take care, darlin'," he said, with a fingertip to eyebrow salute. "Guess if I could leave you with another bit of corn pone advice, it'd be to remember that even though it doesn't look like it now, things really do work out. The trick is just to hang around long enough to see it happen."

CHAPTER 13

S HE PAID WITH HER Amex, took the key and practically flew to her room. Dirty, no luggage, no car, she was a sight, but not the faintest flash of suspicion from the matronly desk clerk. This look must be all too common in Barstow, she guessed.

The room was freezing, a treat for desert drivers. Stripping down, her clothes ended up on the bed (some), and the floor (mostly). The television went on as soon as she passed it, better to have noise than to keep wandering the dusty hallways of her mind.

With blaring bells and sirens of a game show in the background, she jumped in the shower. Dust and dirt soon swirled around her feet, eddies at the tips of her toes, before spiraling down the drain. Water, moisture. Life. That's what it reminded her of. The house had been dry, baked to death from too many baking summers. The air inside the same: parched, used up. A mummy's stale breath.

Finally, when she couldn't feel her skin where the water blasted her, she fumbled for the faucet, cranked it off. Someone had answered a question correctly and applause was rain on a tin roof from the other room.

Wrapped in a towel no thicker than a tissue, sitting on the edge of the bed, she gawked vacantly at the flashing lights, the happy contestants.

What now? It came back, despite the water, the bubbling delight of the game show. Doud was something else. He looked human, sounded human, but he wasn't. He killed, she knew that now. He murdered people. He was immortal. He painted pictures in human blood, or at least he used to.

And he knew where she was. He might come for her: gaping mouth, horrible suction, fevered eyes. She should get away, hit the road. Go back to LA.

Back? Back to what?

She was on the phone to the front desk when someone knocked. "Just a minute," she yelled, hurriedly finishing her clothes-cleaning details.

"Yes?" she said, peering through the peephole.

Doud, distorted by the fish eye: flesh swollen, glossily distended around collar and cuffs, hair mad and patterned with filth, clothes stiff and stained from god knew what. Not the shrunken, dehydrated thing in the dead weeds. Not at all. This was a Doud that'd been partially erased and redrawn, recreated.

She opened the door, invited him in, brought him glass after glass after glass of tepid tap water, rushed him into the bathroom, told him to shower.

After a lengthy, hissing, bubbling and splashing, he came out, also shrouded in cheap terrycloth.

Shelly spoke first: "What do we do now?"

CHAPTER 14

THE FIRST ORDER OF business was clothes. Doud was a priority, because his were in worse shape. Afternoon had dropped away, night taking over, store lights flickering to life.

Hunger. She said she was feeling it; he said he wasn't. They located a fast food place, he waiting in the car while she ran in. Soon, the cloying smell of grease and hot salt mixed with the legacy of her cigarettes in the car. They didn't talk much, or rather she did and he didn't respond.

Why am I waiting? he thought.

Slurping soda, eating her hamburger in great, wolfish bites, or delicately nibbling on fries, she kept her eyes glued on the view out the window, never glancing at him. The way he looked, Doud couldn't blame her.

He's not here. No real evidence, except for the message the monster had passed along, but it was enough. It rang true, made sense. Besides, why go through the trouble of making a messenger if the message was a lie?

"Done," she said, waving an empty cup.

A nod in response, and he cranked up the engine. A few minutes before, sliding through town, they'd seen a mall splashed with the lurid primary colors of chain stores. Retracing the route, he guided them into the white-lined darkness of the parking lot just as encroaching darkness triggered its sodium light, flickering then flooding the area with sickening yellow glow.

"Be right back. Anything special you want?"

"Something basic, durable." He'd already given her his sizes back at the motel.

"Got it," she said, out of the car in a quick bluster of more hot desert air. She didn't need to ask if he wanted to come along. He was hardly presentable, having to crawl back into his dirty clothes after his shower. Driving was okay, but there was no way he could get out.

The parking lot was cheap sodium gold, the town a sparse cascade of other illuminations: the reds, greens and further yellows of a nearby cluster of traffic lights, the aquarium glow from a gas station, fluorescents filtered through thick, bulletproof glass, white from approaching traffic, arterial red from cars departing in the opposite lane. Pretty, but only after dark. The town was a gigantic work of kinetic, abstract art.

Art. Artists. Sergio back in his mind.

Away from Frank's remains, his fury cooled by time and distance, he could think about Sergio again beyond fantasies of snapping him in half, and now look at what he was, had been, with greater clarity.

He'd been on his mind a lot, and not just lately. Yes, the missing assistant director, definitely blood on lace, but even after he'd thought he'd corrected his mistake, thought he'd killed him, Sergio's face, his smell, the feelings, hadn't gone away. Of them all, and there had been quite a few over the long years, none of the others had lingered. Only Sergio.

Blood. The sight of it was the death of a lot of things, the little assistant director—what was his name?—being just one of them. Things like love, hope, and now choice. He had to go, he had to find Sergio.

The monster's message was unmistakable and it made too much sense: Sergio loved the desert, liked the smooth lines of it, the purity of its blasting heat. The idea that there were things that could grow, even prosper, in hell entranced him. Or had, long years ago.

Yet…why the creature?

How had he found out about the house?

A police car roared by, cerulean bursts, crimson flashes. Doud sank into his seat. He must really hate how the world's turned out. It had moved too fast for Sergio, even back in the years of terrifying gas heaters, mountainous steam trains, automobiles like tin toys. Even working for the pictures, he hadn't grasped what nitrate stock, then the talkies, really meant, preferring instead to look backwards rather than forwards.

Backwards, rather than forwards: That night again, still fresh in Doud's mind, at the feet of elephants, gazing out across the fake antiquity of Babylon, the so-much-fainter lights of Hollywood. Back then: A simple sweet soul, kisses at midnight.

Everything changes.

Shelly returned, paper and plastic bags in hand, shop names illegible by angle and sodium lamps. "Hi!" she bubbled, getting in, invigorated by her shopping. "Got some stuff I hope you like. Not exactly Armani, but better than you might think."

"Thank you" he said, voice soft and hollow.

"No problem. What do we do now? I mean, what's the plan? Back to LA? Stay here? You tell me, I do it. I'm kind of in the dark here. More than usual, that is."

Back on the street, he wished he could just drive and never stop. "I don't know what to do," he lied. "I need to think."

"I understand. I just hope you keep me clued in, that's all. I didn't know what to do back there at the house. I'll tell you, though; you're damned lucky I didn't just get out of there and never come back. I almost didn't leave you that note."

"I'm sorry, I didn't mean to get you involved."

"Well, hon, I am. I'm up to the tits in this. I wish I wasn't, but I am. I just wish I knew exactly what's going on. What was that thing back there?"

"Sergio made it…for me to find."

"Well, that answers one question. I guess your ex-boyfriend can do that little breeder trick too. Great. Fantastic. Fuck." She went through her bags, pawing through fabrics, clearly distracting herself. "How the hell could he do that? I thought you said you were the only one that could do that."

"I thought I was." He'd discovered it by accident, and used it more than a few times, always when the loneliness simply got too much for him. But it had always ended with regret, and he'd always had to undo the damage and take back what he'd given them: Screams (from them) and tears (from him), and paintings (afterward). The trick was to drink just enough—not too much, not too little—then force it back, refilling them, changing a man into…whatever the hell Doud was. What Sergio was. He didn't remember telling Sergio how to do it, but then he didn't remember every little detail of their time together. Maybe he'd told him, let slip the secret of making others of their kind. He simply couldn't recall.

"So there could be others out there, huh?" Staring out the window, she said what he'd been thinking: "Anywhere. Anyone. Oh, man."

"I don't think so. He's playing a game. I don't know why. That thing was just a way of delivering a message." Things changed, horseless carriages to Web pages, Sergio, a sweet Italian orchestra to a hideous beast, but making legions of bellowing monsters was just not like him. It didn't make sense. The game (his piece in one corner, Sergio's in the other) was artistic. That made sense.

Or maybe he was lying to himself. Again.

"'A message.' What's the matter with this guy? Never heard of a phone call? Shit. Fuck." She went back to the window, tracking people on the street. "And you dated this guy? I know you were scared of him, but this is something else. God, Doud, you can really pick them."

"He wasn't like this. Before, I mean." *Was he? Really? What didn't I see? What did I miss?* "He changed."

"I'd say so." Rubbing her eyes, she continued. "What happened back there? I just saw, and I'm not too sure what I saw, but it scared me. Oh man, it scared me." Head moving, following men and women on the street of Barstow, she trailed off. "You wanted to eat me, didn't you?"

He didn't respond, just started the car and pulled out of the lot.

Night had completely arrived, not even the hint of day remaining. Barstow blazed in all its neon, fluorescent, incandescent glory. A rainbow at night, a prism fragmented by logos, streetlights, stoplights, headlights, taillights, and more. It was a town defined by small points of illumination, the rest lost to darkness, a suggestion rather than knowledge.

"But you didn't," she said, in a volume and resonance unfamiliar to him. "Thanks."

CHAPTER 15

STOPPING AT AN INTERSECTION, commanded by a bright ruby lens in a dark, hooded housing swinging gently back and forth in a desert breeze he couldn't feel, insulated by the car. "Don't thank me."

"Why not? A few damned hours ago you wanted…you wanted to kill me, but you didn't. I'd say that's worth thanking you for."

Green gave him permission to move on. "I killed someone else, instead of you." His name was Frank McHenry, 45 years old. Was 45 years old. "I don't remember anything about it, but I know I killed him. I was too hungry to know what I was doing." As if that makes a difference.

Chewing her lip for a moment, she went on: "That should scare me, but it doesn't. Okay, not much. I didn't know this other person, but I know that you could have killed me and you didn't. That means something. I know you like to say you're a goddamned monster, but that's bullshit. Sure, you're weird and fucked up, more than most of us, but you try to do the right thing. Your paintings, shit like that. Your boyfriends, too. I get that. Who the hell wouldn't want someone, anyone, in their life? I like to think I'm a pretty good judge of people, honey, and I have to tell you that you're the nicest…whatever the fuck you are I've ever met."

It was her turn to want to reach out, put a hand around his arm.

He didn't deserve it. Body rigid at her touch, tensed, he kept his eyes focused on the road. *You don't understand. You never can, never will.*

"The big thing, and I know you don't want to think about this, is to decide what we're going to do next. If he knew about your house here, then for sure he knows about your place in LA, and probably mine as well. No shit he wants you to go meet him, but I think that's probably the dumbest thing in the world. We could surprise him somehow, trick him into thinking you're being good ol' Doud, but then WHAM, we zap him somehow. We could get a gun. That could help. Or get our hands on something else…something even nastier, though I haven't the foggiest what that could be."

They were about a dozen blocks from the motel, another red light stopping them. A gas station was on the right, a bright island of brilliance, gleaming chrome pumps under the lights. To the left, a pair of golden arches. Couples and families facing each other over colorful blooms of wax paper, smiling as they sipped from straws. Ahead was the rest of the strip, store after store, service after service, until the end of the world.

Red relinquished control, and they cruised off. A man and a woman strolled by, he with a wide-bottomed gait, hand like a ham wrapped delicately around hers.

"Doud? What are we going to do?"

"Needles," he said, more to himself than to her. "'Come to Needles,' is what he said."

"I've heard of it." A bitten-off laugh. "Death Valley Days kind of place, right?" Fumbling with her bag, she pulled out a cigarette and a lighter, lit up. "Okay, so we have a place, but we need to figure out what we're going to do. I don't think we're going to just drive there, right? I mean, that's just what he wants you to do."

They were at the motel. Her room was in the back, shadowed, dark, removed from the glare of the main drag.

Putting the nose of the car right in front of 17, her room, he parked. "I don't even know how much time we've got. He could show up any minute. God, there's something to think about. The way I figure it, he thinks you're going to play his game and go right to him. Put your big dumb head right in the lion's mouth." Stabbing out her cigarette in the car's ashtray, she reached down, grabbed her bags. "But we're not going to do that, right?" Not waiting for an answer, she got out.

Following her, Doud glanced back towards the highway. The view wasn't easy to find, much of the stucco and cement maze of the motel blocking the way, but, tilting, squinting, he was rewarded with a few stray flashes, surges of advertising glow.

"Here you go," she said, handing him a pair of bags. "Like I said, I hope you like them. You should get over to the office and get yourself a room. We've probably got a lot of stuff to do tomorrow, to get ready for all this."

"You're not going," he said, as she put her hand on the knob.

"Of course I am. I have to see it through." She may have looked strong and certain, but there was also a quaver in her voice that spoke more than what she said: fear, sadness...not about the danger, but rather about being left behind.

"No, you don't." He felt calm, the hesitation and complexity that'd been haunting him clearing up, a fog lifting. "I'm sorry. It was stupid of me to bring you along. This has nothing to do with you. Let me finish," he said to her open mouth. "I'm going. You're staying here."

"Damnit, I'm not going to sit here and let you walk right into his fucking mouth..." Her eyes darted suddenly, showing that she'd unintentionally chosen the wrong word. Waving a hand, shooing away the mistake, she tried to start again, slower, more reasonably: "I want to go. You're my friend. We've been through this together so far and I've been okay. I want to help."

"You have, but you're not going. It won't be safe." He couldn't look at her, so he stared out into the soft black night instead. "I started this, I have to finish it. Sergio wants me to come, so I'm going to come. I'm going to kill him, Shelly."

"I know that. But come on, think this through. He's meaner and nastier than you are. You need all the help you can get, even if it's just someone to drive. I know what you've done, but you're not him. You didn't ask to be what you are. You hate it. Fuck, he loves it. Like leaving you that 'calling card.'"

What she was saying made sense. He'd thought the same thing as Frank was trickling through his fingers. But hearing her saying it, a voice not his own, put it right in front of him, in letters too tall to ignore.

Intolerance is gone, except on film. Mr. Griffith is dead. Hollywood is elite restaurants, sushi, fast cars, cell phones, tanning booths, tummy tucks, and power lunches. Everything changes. Everyone changes.

Face it, accept it. He's gone. He's not the man you knew, if you ever knew him. Of all of them, he was one you honestly cared for, the one you had the greatest hopes for. You want what you hoped he'd be, not what he was. "I know that. But I have to go. I have to take care of this. He's my responsibility."

"Wake up. He's a monster. He likes killing people." Dropping her bags, clothing tumbled out, materials on top of materials: cotton, denim, polyester, on the concrete in front of the door.

"Damnit, I'm not a fucking little girl who has to have someone always taking care of her. I can deal with this, okay? I can deal. I can handle it. I've managed to get this far."

He was angry. His pulse raced, his muscles tensed. "Shelly —" he said, voice strained.

"Don't. Just don't. I'm coming and that's all there is to it. Beside the fact that I'm your friend, we're in this together. You and me."

You and me. Together. "No, we're not in this together. You'll never understand. I've had to kill them all. Every time I think I find someone, I have to kill them. But that's not the worst. The worst is knowing I'm just like them. A killer."

Her body stiffened, solid with fear. "I—I understand," she said softly.

"You don't understand. I killed a man today because I was hungry. I could do the same to you, and not be aware of it until I woke up afterward. That's what I am. That's what I've been for a very long time. I kill, that's what I do. That's all I do," he said, stepping towards her. "You can't know. Never," he was yelling, bellowing. Frustration, guilt, shame, fear, anger boiled in his brain. Muscles tensed, his fists knotted into white knuckled balls at his sides. "Come with me and you will die. He'll kill you, or I will."

Doud opened his mouth.

A scream, a compression release, but in, not out. Despite how much he hated himself for doing it, it felt good. It always felt good.

He let slip his hunger's leash. Even though he'd already fed, the need was always there, always eager to consume even more. Wanting and needing were two different things, but not to his belly. Even full, the ecstasy that came with the promise of taking in life, still more fluids, never left.

Kiss me, he thought, as he always did, but unlike every other time, he didn't step forward, didn't take her into his steel-strong arms, didn't clamp his mouth over hers. The monster didn't, because just like with the roofer, unlike with Frank, Doud was in control. Hanging back, he swung open his jaw, opened himself up, and showed her what he really was.

My name is Ernst Doud. I pretend to be many things: an artist, a lover, a man, but this is what I really am.

Howling, shrieking, she dropped, collapsed to the cement walkway. Back against the door, she kicked and jerked, banging hard against the laminated motel room door. Clawed hands flailing out, she scratched, battered, and flailed clumsily at him, body language blaring: GO AWAY!

The tearing octaves of her cries got to him, penetrating even through his bellowing hunger.

Deliberately, painfully, he clamped it down, locked it up, shut the door, closed his mouth. It wasn't easy to do, to put the need away without satiating it. But he kept his concentration on Shelly, pushing against the door with frantic kicks, shrieking, and did it.

Pounding in his ribcage, his heart raced, demanding to be let out. His lungs burned like he'd been inhaling hot ashes.

Hunger stifled, the quiet night of Barstow returning, he heard motel rooms opening, knew there'd be people soon. Time to go.

"I'm sorry," he said, picking up his bags, getting in the car, leaving her behind. Looking up from the dash, he saw her crawl to her feet, up on weakened knees, lean back against the motel room door. Expression tight, but no longer completely rigid with fear, she mouthed his name, but, he too weak and his just-started engine too loud, he couldn't hear her.

Navigating in reverse until he was clear of the breezeway, then shifting into drive, he headed out towards the streaking lights of the highway, all that time never looking back at her, studiously avoiding the tiny form he knew was retreating into the distance.

CHAPTER 16

HE'D ONLY BEEN ON the road for an hour before he had to pull over. Barstow had followed him for a while, the gaudy displays eventually falling behind, to be replaced with the familiar landscape of night driving: tail lights in front, headlights bright in the opposite lanes.

By the time he'd gotten to the freeway, his heart had stopped its bass drumming, a honey-dipped lethargy instead surging over him.

Needles was just two or so hours away, according to the white-on-green signs, but he wasn't going to make it. Not without a break.

Ducking into a convenient rest stop, he switched off the engine. Guilt came at him from an empty passenger seat, bags of clothing. Pragmatism, though, was an easy distraction, so he took advantage of darkness to strip down, change into his new clothes.

In stiff new jeans and a scratchy blue cotton shirt, he reclined the seat. Sleep came quickly. Even with Sergio waiting for him in that desert town, Doud baring his unrelenting hunger at Shelly and then closing his mouth against it, he didn't dream. Thankfully.

He awoke in the morning, cramped from the tight position, especially from his knees being jammed under the steering wheel.

Rubbing the sleep from his eyes, he inspected the little rest stop. Dawn had come up an hour before, revealing his oasis was in the middle of flat dry nothingness, only the freeway behind and before as evidence of anything else in the world.

The desert. Barstow on the edge. Needles in the middle.

Keep going. Don't want to keep him waiting. Rested, refreshed, still full, Doud got back on the highway.

Normally an hour wasn't a long time, but this time it felt stretched, distorted to at least twice that as he drove. The silence in the car was at first a novelty, then claustrophobic. He didn't really miss her nervous chatter, but Shelly had kept his mind from wandering off to bad territories, at least some of the time. Without her, he sped down a dark, frightening avenue: Sergio. The monster. Frank, dust and ashes.

Shelly, Shelly, Shelly.

He turned on the radio.

But between bursts of static as he spun the dial, her screams cut through. Tears burned his eyes.

Needles, a sign said, one mile.

Sergio didn't cry, Sergio only laughed. Sergio didn't regret or try to apologize. Sergio took and killed.

He'd never been to Needles, and cruising around the small town, he saw absolutely no reason to come back. Barstow had paved over its past, covered it up with as much convenience as possible; mini-malls rather than ghost towns, dealerships instead of museums. Barstow resented being left behind in the wake of its chrome and fast-paced sister to the east, Los Angeles, and so tried to catch up, in its cowboy hat and 4x4 kind of way.

Needles, though, took pride in its antiquity. Rather than be dissatisfied with its backwardness, it inflated its historical self-esteem. An unequivocal sign of that was a covered wagon proclaiming the town's name in Gold Rush typography, an artificial landmark he circled several times to get his bearings.

Having arrived, he had no idea what he was looking for. The town wasn't very big, just a point on a map compared with the larger smudge of Barstow. Sergio, it seemed, shouldn't be hard to find. But after covering a majority of the town, he was confused. The invitation had been clear, written as it had in a once-human life, but what good was a message if it didn't lead anywhere? Cruising the streets, he kept a quarter of his sight on the sparse traffic of pickup trucks and SUVs and the remaining three quarters for any sign of his old boyfriend.

And he tried not to think of Shelly, and her screams.

Hardware, convenience, tack, book stores, gas stations, bars, markets: the usual kind of town view out his windshield, albeit with an architectural flair for what used to be. But absolutely nothing in the wagon wheels, coils of rope, spurs, 49ers seemed to be the next page of the message: "Come to Needles."

Three hours later, he parked, got out. As his shoes met sidewalk, he finally understood that he really was in the middle of a desert. Leaving the carefully conditioned air of his car, he felt the inherent truth of the cliché, "walking into an oven." Open the door, put your face in. That was Needles.

He hated it. Breathing steadily, he tried to reconcile his cooled body to the roasting air. How can Sergio live here?

Life was wet to Doud. It was what he ate, what kept him going, and what, if he didn't get enough of it, changed him from a "nice little fag" to a ravenous mouth. To be in a place that competed with his personal hunger, sucked the liquid life out of everything, was terrifying. The desert was determined, relentless, endlessly thirsty, totally uncaring, and, just like his hunger, apparently ageless.

Spotting a phone booth under a convenience store's overhang, he crossed melting asphalt only to find the pages, both white and yellow, missing. The local operator couldn't help him either; Sergio Insana wasn't listed, nothing even close. He hung up, unsure what to do. The local newspaper was an idea, but not yet.

Thinking of a newspaper brought up seeing Sergio's name in print, reminded him of the card, the one with the two numbers, the one Sergio had given Shelly.

He remembered it being in his hand, the name in neatly printed letters. He also remembered putting it down on a table, and not picking it back up.

It was stupid, but instantly he knew why he'd done it. The card, bearing that name, had been a tangible reminder. Holding it, back in his apartment, there'd been an itch, an ache, just like the one that still haunted his painting hand; a comforting act denied. If he'd kept it, he would have been tempted to pick up a phone, any phone, and dial just to hear his voice.

He damned himself. If he'd been smart, kept the card, a call could have given him a clue, but just as quickly, trying to steady his nerves, he reassured himself that the message had been unmistakable: "Come to Needles." The next step in the game.

He started to walk. He knew he could cover a lot more ground by driving, swaddled in air conditioning, but being on foot, he thought, might bring him, and what he was there for, into focus.

Focus, yes, but also a distorted, paranoid perception he quickly realized: a darkened storefront made him anxious, visualizing a leap from the shadows. A narrow alley made him fretful, seeing Sergio there, grinning with his insatiable mouth, radiating power. Any sharp sound—car door slam, burst of salsa, honking horn—was a shock, a jolt, the first chord of an attack.

The heat was gone, forgotten, burnt out of him by every blind corner, every noise, every instant of contact with the tanned people of Needles. Blinking away sweat, it made him duck under every awning, propelled him under every piece of available shade.

Stopping at a corner, lethargic from the heat, he looked this way, that, down and then up, each street. *He's here. He's got to be here.* He wiped his slick forehead with the back of a hand. But where?

CHAPTER 17

"You look like a fella who's looking for someone." Tall, skin sunned to a buttery glow. Wheat hair, combed only by hot desert wind. Simple jeans, worn at the knees, and a blue cotton shirt. "Or waiting for someone. Either way, he must be damned special for you to be out in this god-awful heat."

He was leaning with arms folded against the bulging fender of a slate gray pickup, showing rows of clean, white teeth.

Doud jumped when he spoke. This man, actually seeing, speaking to him, was a reminder that there was a world beyond his myopic fears. Shaken, he grinned nervously, sputtering, "Oh…looking. I'm supposed to meet somebody."

"Someone I might know? I may not be the most socially connected of individuals, but I know more than my fair share." The teeth stayed visible, his golden skin creased into easy laugh lines. The arms remained folded, hinting at wide, strong shoulders beneath the shirt.

Panic flashed through Doud's mind, his body reacting with quick tension to his muscles. But as he looked in the man's eyes, saw the glow in his cheeks, his distinctive nose, he decided that his fear was unwarranted. Leaning back against his truck, he didn't appear to be hungry, a starving like the thing in Barstow. "Maybe. A friend asked me to meet him here, in town, but didn't say where."

"Excuse me for saying so, but he doesn't sound like much of a friend." The happy creases widened, revealing even more teeth.

"He's not, but I need to find him."

"Like I said, I do know a fair number of folks," the man said, drifting into a near-twang. "I might just be able to point you in the right direction."

Weak, light-headed, Doud's head was stuffed with cotton, packed with gauze. Just a man, he's just a man. Panic lifting, fear parting, he returned the grin. Just a man. Delight, elation. Nothing but a man.

No longer alone on the boiling streets of Needles, where every sound was Sergio's, every corner hid his face, every smell was his scent, every vibration was his step, Doud was relieved.

Relieved, yes. That was it. He wanted to be back to normal: his little apartment, his art, jars of peanut butter, his usual level of self-pity and loneliness, bad movies, watching the world age and change, as he didn't. Talking to this man, who just seemed to be interested in helping, or just wanted to chat, was a welcome dose of typical.

"His name is Insana," Doud said, and thoughts of 'typical' evaporated. "That's his last name. His first name is Sergio."

"Insana?" repeated the other man, rolling it on his tongue, pronouncing it correctly each time. "Insana, Sergio Insana. Oh, man, that doesn't ring any sort of bell. Up here we got a lot of Bobs, Larrys, Stus, Stanleys, and quite a few Miguels, and Hay-sus-es, but sad to say no one with that particular name. What's this fellow do? That sometimes helps. You know, like the way mechanics know every other mechanic in town."

"He's an artist."

"An artist? That narrows it down some. Bad news though, 'cause I dabble a bit myself, and I still don't recall anyone with that name. You one too?"

"Used to be. Not anymore."

"That's a shame. See, I say that once you've got it, you've always got it. Guess for you, though, it just needs a rest, huh? Anyway, like I said, that name doesn't ring for me, but tell you what. I've got some local magazines and stuff, back at my place. What say I dig them out and give you a call. If he's put brush to paper or hand in clay, then he's sure to show up in some of those things."

Unsure of what was happening, suspicions ran through his mind. One of Sergio's creatures? Better trained, recently fed? A trick? A move in the game?

Then why the pleasant chat?

The other man never stopped grinning, but left his position against the old gray truck to walk up to Doud. "Where are you staying? Give me your number and I'll call you after I get through them. If you say he's here, and he's one of us 'artistic types,' sure he's gotta be in there. I'll track him down for you, no problem."

He'd wanted it to get back to the way it had been: his little apartment, his art, jars of peanut butter, his usual level of self-pity and loneliness, bad movies, watching the world age and change as he didn't, and looking into another man's eyes to enjoy that special, silent communication between them.

That was it. This handsome desert rat wasn't hungry, not in Doud's ferocious way, but had been savoring him with that other kind of craving.

I am, I hope you are too, was the silent communication between them.

Doud finally returned the smile. "That would be nice. Thank you. I'm not staying anywhere right now. I could call you when I find a place," he said, finding the language easy, natural, comforting.

"No problem! Like I said, we've got to stick together, right?" His hand landed on Doud's shoulder, a firm, playful impact. "I'll go right back to my digs and go through those old magazines. If he's anywhere, he's got to be in one of those. Besides, I know quite a few of the paint-splatterers and mud-throwers around here. I'll find your friend, come hell or high water."

The hand was warm, firm and it didn't move. *What am I doing?* But the answer was clear, concise, all too simple. So straightforward, he knew it before the question was completely formed in his mind. He was tired (so tired) of it all and this was such an easy, well-remembered dance.

Home. Familiarity. Just below his awareness, he understood he was being selfish, knew he should be out, searching, searching, searching, searching for Sergio but the shocks of the last few days had been too dramatic, too intense so he was dramatically, intently escaping them all with this flirtation. "Thanks. I'm very grateful. Perhaps I could take you out to dinner sometime?"

Laughing: "Hell, man, I haven't done anything yet. Tell you what. You're the stranger in town; let me take you out. This town's got quite a few places for some decent eats, but there's no way anyone new would know the good from the bad."

With the belly-rocking sound, the hand came away. Losing the contact was painful. Doud wanted it back. "I'd like to. Really. But I have to find him, the man I'm looking for. It's really important."

"Then I'll tell you what." Eyes narrowing in contemplation. "There's no way I could claim to be as good a cook as some of the nicer eateries in town, but I can sling some pretty good hash. My place is just a few miles outside of town. Come on over and we'll go over those magazines and stuff, and I'll put my good ol' brain to work trying to figure out where this Sergio guy is. How's that for a plan? Work for you?"

Kind, funny, and rugged; Doud liked him. Not attractive, not really, but a face full of character you could look at for a long time. He wanted to touch him, feel his rough, thick skin, rub his palm across the top of his head and savor the hair tickling through his fingers.

This rough-edged man with his dazzling teeth, brilliant dentistry, was someone new and fresh, a throaty voice he hadn't heard before, saying there still might be a chance.

"I—I'd like that," Doud, said, blushing at his stutter, coughing into his fist to cover it up. "Excuse me. That would be fine. A little company would be nice."

"Done deal, and don't worry, we'll find your friend. I'm the kind of guy who looks a problem dead on and says 'you're going down,' and means it. One way or another I'll help you track down this no-account so and so. Promise." Brown hand on the handle, he stood a bit straighter. "Hey, I just put a couple of twos together and got a four. You drove, right? Want to follow me, or leave your car here and just pick it up later?"

"Leave it here. I'll come back for it, if you don't mind driving." Many things left behind, perhaps picked up later, perhaps never reclaimed, the car just one of them. Worry bellowed in the back of his mind, but he ignored it, concentrating instead on the play of muscles and skin in the other man's face, the way he moved in his durable clothes.

What am I doing?

"Not at all," the fellow said opening the truck's passenger side door. "Hop in. It's not new but it's the best one there is."

What the hell am I doing?

The inside of the truck was an even hotter oven, nearer a furnace. The seats, black leather, were worn down to the consistency of his new friend's desert-shaded skin. Old, the truck was still lovingly maintained. For Doud, it was uncomfortable, this kind of obsessive preservation. The antiques in his apartment may have been ancient by many standards, but their wear and tear was a gentle reminder that Doud was living now, the scars and damage familiar and comfortable reminders of his real age. This truck, though, was too immaculate, too perfect. It was like it'd been transported from an era of chrome tailfins, whitewalls, and Elvis. Those years had been safe and relaxing for Doud, he having just survived Europe and the horrors of the war, but it was still disturbing, disorienting, like he'd been swept back to that decade.

I'm going to find Sergio. Justification.

"All set?" his friend asked, starting the truck. It sounded like a boat engine; a throbbing, pounding cycle. "Off we go." Shifting, they merged with the light traffic. A few ponderous twists of the huge, stiff wheel and they were heading towards the edge, then out of town, heading out to the pure straight line of the distant desert.

You haven't won, you bastard. I'll show you, I'll show you that there's still a chance. I'll find someone—

The interior of the truck was loud, though not so loud they couldn't talk, but neither one said anything. They knew where they were going, and why, so it seemed that nothing really needed to be said. But as they passed a sign (Now Leaving Needles) Doud realized he'd forgotten something important. Leaning across the seat, he called out. "So sorry! My name's Doud. Ernst Doud."

The driver laughed again; a good, solid, true sound. "Nice to meet you, Mr. Doud. Pleasure to make your acquaintance. My name's Vince. Vincent Ferris. Though some people have been known to call me 'Galahad.'"

CHAPTER 18

S HE HADN'T SLEPT. THAT was part of it.

But still, when dawn lit the windows of yet another motel room, she felt strange, disconnected, like she'd become someone else during the night. The world hadn't changed. Parting the dirty yellow curtains and peering out, she saw it was still Barstow. Same cowboy hats, same jeans, same dirty SUVs rumbling by on the main highway. Same painfully dry air. Same smell of exhaust and dust.

Same outside, but not same inside. It was like one of her poles had been switched. Plus now a minus, or the other way around.

This new version, this flipped-over self, was still hooked, though. Despite the warnings on the cardboard sign folded into a stable little cardboard 'A' on the table, she lit up. A fleeting worry made her scan for a smoke detector, but then, with a satisfying puff, she realized she simply didn't care. If it shrieked, she'd either knock it down or flash a 'who me?' grin at whoever showed up. Irate motel managers, firemen, cops, all of them part of the everyday things from the common, ordinary side. Not hers.

It was nothing to worry about, especially after what she'd seen.

Remarkably, she wasn't tired. The entire idea of sleep eluded her. Shutting her eyes, she tried to recapture what it had felt like, being tired, but it just wouldn't come.

It would though, eventually. That part of her, the flesh and bone, the muscles and tendons, her brain, the remaining five bucks in chemicals hadn't changed. But for now, her mind, the lighting in that gray oozy stuff, was seeing things differently.

Walking over to the window, gazing out the window, taking another drag, she absently followed someone walking down the street, amazed for a second by the absolute dullness of it: the way the woman's legs scissored back and forth, the way her arms swung, also back and forth. Just another middle-aged woman in sweat pants, walking home after a run.

She doesn't know. Doesn't have a clue what's out there.

Shelly knew. It hadn't been when she figured out that her little gay friend painted pictures in human blood. Not even after she'd seen Doud in the weeds, emaciated, primal, starving, and knowing that he'd seen her, as food. Steps along the way, sure, but none of that had switched it around, plus to minus, minus to plus. No, that had come last night.

Doud, screaming hunger. Mouth wide, distended, pulling at her, that needy, horrible, gasping maw towards her.

That had done it. Right then. He wasn't her little gay friend, the guy who grinned when she prattled on and on with some silly story, or bitched about having a bad day. Not the quiet man, who she always knew, somehow, was really listening to her. Not the pal she took to the movies, sharing Milk Duds and popcorn, and whose eyes brightened and shone, polished buttons in the dark, during flickering scenes of loss or redemption, or laughed like a startled flock of birds when Groucho wiggled his black painted brows. Not the dinner date telling evocative tales, each phrase like a perfectly prepared entree of meals in Paris, Bucharest, London, and Madrid, and making her wish she could have been at those tables, feasting on those fantastic courses.

Last night, Doud wasn't any of that. Last night, she'd seen what he really was.

Grounding out her smoke on the counter, making a matching crisp black crater among others who'd disobeyed the sign, she stepped back from the window.

It didn't seem all that long, but when she actually did the math, she couldn't move. Had she really known him *that* long? It'd been just after she'd opened her gallery, a month or so after. That would make it…six years? The number was surprising, and not just because of the way time had changed for her, sitting as she was in the start of middle age, but because six years seemed like more than enough time to get to know someone. Six years. Nothing at all in six whole years.

The paintings, of course, should have been a *dead* (she smiled wryly to herself) giveaway, but they weren't. Even if she'd doubted his blushing explanations of cow, goat and sheep blood, she knew the way her mind would have gone: who would be so absolutely bonkers to paint in *human* blood and fluids and then go around pedaling the work to Melrose galleries? They were in LA, after all, but even the land of flakes and nuts had its limits.

Blindness…odd in a gallery owner. She hadn't *wanted* to see. He'd been refreshing, simple and honest. Most of the 'creative types' she dealt with were better at wearing a costume, putting on a show than really being an artist. Not Doud; he'd been different. First of all, he was gay, he was her own age—

No, not that. He hadn't been honest—and was certainly not her age.

Flipside, reversed, twisted, mirror-side, plus switched with minus, turned over. Even with her new perspective, she couldn't connect her friend, the painter, a fucking contemporary of Abraham Lincoln, with that thing that had screamed hunger.

The world was fuzzy, this side of things. Doud's side of things.

She stared at the bags of clothes she'd bought; getting dressed would help, give her something to do.

Even popping off tags and pulling off labels, though, she kept wandering back. *What was he?* More importantly, had he ever been, and was he now, her friend?

Flapping out a pair of jeans, hands busy, mind still racing she puzzled, weighed, figured…and puzzled, weighed, and figured still more.

Being the gregarious extrovert that she was, she'd had more than her fair share of companions, serious as well as silly, but there was something about Doud that had stayed with her. Everyone else was on the way somewhere else: other gallery owners who really wanted to paint, waiters wanting to be screenwriters, screenwriters wanting to direct, directors wanting to be sex machines, sex machines who wanted depth. None of them where they wanted to be.

He'd be there, standing or sitting or talking or eating or just watching a movie. At the time, she thought he'd been mature, settled in, accepting of himself. She had a sudden memory of one night: after eating at a fair (only fair) Thai place, they'd run off to see a flick, something Shakespearian but modernized, tweaked, into a kind of Nazi England. She hadn't liked it, preferring her classics classical, her balconies to be balconies, her Romeos not looking like Juliets, and said so.

He'd come out smiling. It wasn't rare for him to do that, but that time there'd been an extra quality in his expression, not just a disarming smile, or a wry smile, or a slight smile; more like it'd revealed something inside him. She'd kidded him, saying that he just had a major hot-on for the lead. Tenor soft and almost lost, he'd said: "It's the same story, but a different time." Then he'd covered by agreeing that the actor had been very 'nice', which was what he called anyone Shelly said was 'fuckable.'

Flipside now; she saw where that glow had come from. For him, who'd seen men go off to fight the Confederacy, who'd seen men go off to fight Hitler, who'd seen men go off to die in Vietnam…all of that was just the same show, only the stages being different. Seeing that classic story, in a so-unique style, had been reassuring: the play always remained the thing, the Bard's language beautiful no matter where, and when, performed.

What is he? She was dressed. *Hair's a mess.* Checking herself out in the mirror, flicking brown curls with her fingertips, she added to herself: *What is he to me?*

Grabbing her purse, she went out, closing the door behind her. Next order of business: the front desk, to pay for another night.

Even though she couldn't follow him, at least not yet, there was still something she could do.

She could get some answers.

CHAPTER 19

THE MOTEL WASN'T THRILLED with her staying another night. The wrinkled prune behind the desk's steel gray eyes flashed fear and anger when she walked in, but an AMEX opened any number of doors, or kept ajar those that some preferred closed.

Signing the slip, she promised to be gone in the morning, but after one last favor: a cab or shuttle, anything with wheels. After the call was made, the acknowledgment that it would be there shortly given, she tossed "Thanks so much for understanding" over her shoulder and walked out.

After a short stroll, she was by the curb, on the shore of the main drag, to wait for her ride. Shielding her eyes against the hard glare from passing windshields, as well as stationary windows, she tried to pick out the cab, not sure what such a thing would look like in Barstow, California.

Even though she was beginning her new trip a different trip stayed in her mind. So many dinners, so many receptions, so many gallery openings, so many parties, so many times they'd been together, but they'd never talked like they had on the trip up. Trying to remember exactly what he'd said about himself, she came up with barely a handful of information.

Her wave started, then stopped with the arrival of what she guessed was a taxi, but was really a yellow sedan with a roof rack. Okay, time to face facts: she knew she was just a touch self-centered, but Jesus, how could she not have seen, or suspected, that the man who'd sat across tables from her, who'd joked with her, who'd shook his head at 'modern' films was anything but kosher?

Was she that oblivious? Another sedan. Another roof rack? In response to her whistling and waving, the taxi pulled over. *Thank god; a sign of civilization.*

She told the driver to drive, just drive. She didn't know the address, but she had a pretty good sense of direction. Silent, the cabbie pulled into traffic, heading where she gestured.

Sure, she was a 'mouthy broad,' as one of her boyfriends had called her, but that wasn't *all* she was. Mouth, yeah, but she had eyes, and she'd seen something in Doud, something that'd elevated him from what she'd known of the world.

"Turn right here." Under a roughly knit charcoal cap, she didn't know if her driver was a him, her, or even an it. Another monster like Doud, or something even stranger?

"This is it," she said, some mile or two later. As they pulled over, she produced some bills from her purse. "Here you go." She passed over a twenty.

"Thanks," the cabbie said, destroying *his* mystery. Nothing but an old, unshaven man, with a nose like an exotic vegetable, she observed as he passed back her change. Getting out into the hot, gritty air, she slammed the door harder than she intended, the metal-on-metal bang startling her.

A few hot feet down the unpaved road, Doud's house was a flattened triangle under a too-blue sky. She didn't want to go back to the place (the last time had been bad enough, thank you very much) but didn't have any other options.

For anyone else it wouldn't have been a long walk, in time or distance, but for her it was hours and miles, not feet and seconds. The tremble with each rapid heartbeat was her pulse in her neck.

The house got bigger and bigger as she approached it. The front door was shut. Had she shut it? Searching memory, she believed she did. Not knowing made her pulse that much more flighty. What if she had left it open? Who'd closed it? Was there another roaring, hungry, waiting *thing* on the other side?

Her hand was on the knob. She didn't want to, not at all, but she still gripped as hard as she could, hand sweaty, and turned. It wasn't locked, and that made her feel better: yes, she'd closed it, but without a key she hadn't been able to lock it.

Inside, the house was cool. Not dark and shaded enough to be cold, just gently chilly. It seemed to smell even dustier, moldier than the last time, too. Swinging the door closed behind her, she looked towards the living room, then back toward the kitchen. The hole was still there, a lath and plaster rimmed gap in an otherwise smooth and featureless exterior wall. *Was that only yesterday?* Staring at it, she wasn't as frightened as she thought she'd be. She really had crossed to the other side. Scared, yes, but she could just as easily have been terrified (*shit, is this bravery?*). Up to the hole, daring herself to peer down at the field of weeds.

Doud had been down in that field. No, that wasn't correct. Not him, only his hunger.

Still not right. There'd been enough of him left to run away from her.

She moved away from the hole and back into the cool darkness of the house. Another question: why had he run? What had stopped him? Still no answers. Time to start looking for some.

After two hours she had to admit that the house did have some answers, just not very many, at least not that she could find on the first floor. First of all, it had been very affordable back in the 'teens. No basement, an ancient kitchen upgraded to frayed wiring and cheap gas lines. Not a good combination. What with the lingering smell of gas, she decided that switching on the lights wasn't such a good idea, so she ended up poking through cabinets in near darkness. Aside from the living room and dining room, the ground floor was empty. There were only a few simple pieces of furniture, and some obviously inexpensive rugs to cover the hardwood floor.

The upstairs wasn't quite as bare. Two bedrooms and a small bathroom, barely a toilet and sink. One bedroom, the one facing the road and the sunrise, was as empty as downstairs. *What the hell was Doud thinking?* She wondered as she walked from room to room. The house was more than empty. It was vacant. That fact alone said quite a bit; Doud had been scared. He'd run. This place, empty and dusty, absent even the hint of a personality, had been a kind of home. A place to run to, just not a very inviting one.

The back bedroom, though, was full of boxes. Three stacks of three. *Now we're getting somewhere.* Popping the wrinkled tape on the nearest one, she folded back greasy cardboard flaps. Before anything showed, she imagined books, diaries, possibly photos. More grainy sepia revelations, like those he'd shown her back in LA? Doud as a young man, Doud with his young arms around Lincoln, Doud and Hemingway, a painting of Moscow in flames, or was that older than he was?

Blankets. Cans of food, some of them decades old by the designs on the labels. Spam. Giggling softly she held the tin up to a beam of sunlight. *Not exactly a gothic mansion. Got to work on your sense of style…and you call yourself an artist?*

It took her the better part of an hour, but she finally managed to get through all of them. Doud's stash held no surprises. More canned food, some old art magazines from the fifties, with some pictures that may or may not have been Doud's, and a battered cigar box full of buttons and dull coins.

Who the hell are you? How can you be alive for so long and not have anything to show for it?

Ready to leave, head back to the motel to wait, or even (sadness, then an ache) go back to LA, she glanced back into the room, seeing wallpaper, stained by mold and god-knew-what-else, into the map of some yellowish, brownish world. In the middle of it, a painting.

It was a landscape. A watercolor. Not a great range, just a few shades. Whistler, his *Nocturne in Black and Gold*, and images of the Thames came to mind. Subtle. She didn't know where the scene was, but that didn't matter. It was a view of anywhere there'd been water, buildings, fog, piers, and a low sun. It made her feel odd, like she was peeking through a keyhole at something intensely private.

No diaries, no scrapbooks, but she'd found the painting. That was enough.

It wasn't just antique (stale, dusty, fragile, faded) but instead *perfected*. A young man couldn't have painted it, nor could an old man. Only Doud could have painted it; a man who'd seen more sunsets, more fog, more seas, than anyone. A man who'd had time enough to get it right. A technique built up over decades and decades and decades.

The more you have, the less you want to lose. Had he said that or was it the painting speaking? Who needed snapshots with Roosevelt, Gandhi's autograph, a Picasso sketch, when *that* was inside you, the vision and perspective of so many years?

No wonder he's scared, no wonder he's so alone. Forcing herself, she looked away from the painting. Her face felt strange. Chilly. Hand to cheeks, fingers coming away wet. The tears, threatening all day, had finally arrived.

God, that's horrible. To be able to do that, see so damned much, and never forget you have to kill people to do it.

She didn't have all of it, maybe only part of the answer, but she was close, like it had brushed by her ear.

Back down the stairs. A car. She'd have to get one somehow. There had to be a rental place in town.

The door was open. Had she closed it? She *had* closed it. A board creaked to her left, near the shadowed living room, the dining room, that gaping hole overlooking dead weeds. She wasn't alone.

"Hello." Musical instruments, tones of opera.

Oh, shit.

"I didn't expect to find you here," Sergio said, stepping out of the soft darkness.

CHAPTER 20

WHAT THEY SAID ON the road wasn't really important. They followed the same route as before, no detours or sidelines in their conversation, Doud looking for Sergio, Vince offering help, and offering the possibility of other things as well.

In the passenger seat, Doud found himself slipping away, having to ask, again and again, what Vince had just said, the empty horizon of the vacant desert drawing his mind into quiet contemplation.

"Gathering some serious wool, buddy?" Vince said, glancing over with a grin.

"Life's been…complicated lately."

"Oh, I know that score, that's for sure. Nothing worse than having something you thought was simple get all wild on ya. One day you know every highway in the county, the next there's this bend you never knew was there and you're lost." He'd been looking at Doud, but the highway demanded his attention. "Been down that weird road too many times before myself."

Suddenly embarrassed, Doud grinned back weakly. It had been too long. He was rusty, needy. Red-faced, he matched Vince's view forward. "I really appreciate your help."

"Glad to! Not to brag, but if your friend's in these parts, and he's had anything to do with painting, or sculpting, or anything else like, then we should be able to find him. For all this damned big emptiness"—he gestured to the flat dry desert—"it's a damned small town. No one can pass gas out here without a dozen people knowing what you had for dinner."

Charming. Staring at the desert, doubt and hesitation returned. *What am I doing here?* He knew what he should be doing. That was as plain as the single stroke horizon: find Sergio. But in his mind, the process was anything but simple.

Shelly and leaving LA, for instance. Had he done the right thing, dragging her along? He had, but also accepted that his decision had less to do with protecting her than not wanting to be alone. Had he done the right thing, going to Barstow? He hadn't, the monster's presence proved that. Sergio was way ahead of him. How many more moves yet to come? A frightening prospect.

Frightening, bringing his mind back to Shelly. Had he done the right thing, scaring her like that?

Rationalization: had to leave her behind, make her understand, show her the reality of the situation.

Leave her behind…his face flushed. No, no, no. Had it all been part of the game, to make him do exactly that?

An image: fast, all too real, completely unbidden. Shelly returning to the house, wandering dusty hallways, opening closets, peering into corners, picking up dirty glasses in the kitchen, and looking out the hole at the trampled circle of crushed weeds below.

A knock at the door. She, walking back down the musty hall. Her hand on the knob. Opening.

Sergio.

He steps towards her, grabs her, holds her tight.

And kisses her, lips over hers, an unbreakable seal. She tries to fight, can't.

He lets loose the vacuum, his hunger, and begins to feed. First the fluid, the liquid life of her: blood, bile, lymph, saline, all of it, sucking into himself. She shrinks, screaming into his sucking maw. She wrinkles, her bones creaking and breaking from the pressure; her eyes shrivel and submerge into her groaning skull.

Until dusk and desiccated skin, a few fragments of powdery bone, a tangle of hair, is all that's left.

No, no, no. Rubbing the back of his neck, Doud tried to massage away the imagery.

"What's wrong? Looks like you got an attack of the queasies. Something you ate? I'd say it might be my driving, but this is a damned straight road. I've barely touched the wheel since we left town."

No. It didn't make sense. If Sergio had wanted Shelly, he could have taken her anytime, like back at her gallery.

Easy, easy, easy…a chant of relaxation. "I'm okay. Just thinking of him again."

"I hear you, really I do. Look, I know I've been batting my big brown eyes at you ever since we met and I definitely think we have what some folks call a 'connection', but I'm not bullshitting you, Mr. Doud, when I say that I'm damned sure I have something back at my place that will put you on the right track to find this friend of yours. I can all but promise that. Honestly."

"Thank you," he said, feeling like he could take this stranger's hand, reassure himself, but didn't. It wasn't time for that… Not yet. Gazing ahead, the horizon still lurked out the windshield, the feeling of it all being unfinished returning.

Sergio, and hate boiled in his stomach. Something definitely disagreed with him. "But he's not my friend. Sergio is definitely not my friend."

CHAPTER 21

"IT's not much," Vince said, steering them down an unpaved road. "But here we are." Truck bucking over pot and kettle holes, Doud locked a hand to the dash to keep from bouncing on the cracked upholstery.

Two cheap aluminum windows set in a single story cinder-block house. Facing out across the blasted landscape of the desert, its view was broken only by the short, cratered access road. Nothing had been painted, or changed in any way from the boxes it had been shipped in. "Always liked building models when I was a kid," Vince said, pulling up in front. "Same idea, I guess. Different scale."

The place had no personality. It may well have been built by, and for, heavy equipment. Completely unremarkable, and totally utilitarian. "It's nice," Doud said, not sure if it really was a lie or just an understatement.

"You're too kind," Vince said, getting out. "Really. I know it's just a box, but it's my box. That's what I like best about it."

Following, the heat hitting him in the face, breaking him into instant sweat, Doud noticed that the house also blocked the only natural feature on the otherwise featureless plain. Not enough that it's a palace of the dull, but it masks the unique as well.

"It really is nice," he said, peering around the great gray bulge of the truck, searching out Vince's face. Finding it, they shared a wide, honest grin.

"It's shit, be honest," Vince said, heading towards the door, putting out a gangly arm to Doud. "But it's cheap, quiet, and the view is something else. Besides, I like being close to that rock back there. My little box being in the shadow of the only irregular thing out in this damned regular desert. Kinda cool."

The rock was a miniature of its much smaller, red kin in Australia: a great lump of yellow earth dropped (or shoved up) in the middle of the vacant expanse of the hot, barren flats. Vince's house was right in its shadow.

"Doesn't look it, but we're still in Needles. There's actually a sliver of town on the other side of the rock. We passed it on the way in, but you probably missed it."

He had missed it, but didn't say. It bothered him that he hadn't been paying attention. *What else have I missed?* Not responding to Vince's offer of an arm around his shoulder, he trotted behind the tanned man.

Digging into his jeans, Vince brought out a small key ring, bright silver dancing in the sun. "I don't know what your studio is like, but for me I like one with lots of sun and with access to lots of raw materials. One thing for this place, it's got both in spades."

"I don't work anymore. I had to give it up," he said. Chilled air from inside blew around his ankles from the open door. It felt good.

"I'm sorry to hear that," Vince said, inside the darkened, heavily air conditioned interior that bid him to come in. "I like to say that it's something you got or you don't. You can't pick it up or give it away. That's what I say, anyway."

What do you know? Bitterness stiffening his face. *What do you know about anything?*

Lights switching on, Doud saw that the interior was the same: unfinished, common, mass-produced. To the right, a kitchen with white Formica tiles on the floor, the pale monolith of an old-style fridge, the dark stars of a range.

The main room was a box. A plastic-covered couch, thick clear wrapping over yellow and brown corduroy. A folding TV tray was set up on one end, holding up a faintly buzzing electric clock and a cracked, baby-shit-yellow-shaded lamp. The couch faced an up-to-date collection of entertainment gear: wide screen set, DVD player, and stereo piled on a cracked, crushed-from-the-weight footlocker.

The floor could have been painted cement, or still more cheap Formica, but he couldn't tell through the soles of his shoes. Barely lit, mostly dark (the lamp not being lit), the home's only light came from the back wall, a floor-to-ceiling sliding glass door. Past it, he saw where the great stone met the desert, the backyard in its shadow.

"No place like home. But then this isn't really my home; just a place to eat food, drink beer, watch some tube, sleep, that kind of stuff. But you know what I'm talking about."

"Pardon me?" Going from dry, hot air to mechanically chilled air, from too bright sunlight to a shadowy box had disoriented him. "I'm sorry, what do you mean?"

"Okay, I know you hung up your art and all, but I bet you know. This is just a place. But out here, this is where I really live. Come on out and tell me it doesn't remind you of somewhere."

Sliding aside the big glass door, Vince returned to bright light from dark. "The materials may not be the same, but I'll betcha the vibes will be clear as day."

Behind him, the air conditioning tagging along like a pack of small, chilled dogs around his ankles, Doud had to admit Vince was right. He did recognize it.

Plain cement patio, poured right up to the rocky slope of the massive boulder. A rusty folding chair.

That wasn't what he recognized. "Yes," he said to Vince's happy expression. "It seems familiar."

Against the back wall of the house were a half dozen plywood sheets held up by raw pine sawhorses, their edges still toothed with splinters from sloppy cuts. Under them, plastic buckets stacked on plastic buckets, a paint store spectrum, all smeared by grey, white, dark brown clay. Around the buckets were jars, a clustered miscellany of sizes and shapes of old fruit, pickle, jam, and olive glass bottles, their only commonality being full of soil.

An artist's space. The rest of the house was empty, bare, featureless, because the artist didn't live there. He ate there, slept there, rested there, but that wasn't living. Here, in the shade of the rock, with these tools, these raw materials, was where Vince lived.

It wasn't pleasant being in Vince's workspace because it was a solid, real, reminder of what Doud had left behind, several hundred miles away.

"There, you see. Told you it would take one to know one. Might not be the same kind of stuff, but this is the same kind of place, right? Yeah, I know, you said you don't do it anymore, but doesn't this remind you of when you did?"

Face away from Vince's wide, bright grin, to glare again at his outdoor studio, he fought to control a frown, make it less obvious. *Yes it does.*

Near the rock, away from the house, was a small kiln; a squat dome of broken bricks, gaps filled with sloppy mortar. A heavy iron door ajar, showing a charcoal black interior. Behind it, leaning against the rise of the rock, was a cluster of gas cylinders, dust and spider-web hazy.

Vince was right next to him and Doud was hotter, warmer than he'd been in the truck. Despite his flush of anger and pity, he wanted Vince's arm around him.

"Now I'm not one to dig for compliments," Vince said, a throaty whisper. "In fact I really wish I had the strength to just stand here and silently hope, but," he chuckled, "I'm just not as tough as I thought I was, so I have to ask. What do you think?"

Above the tables, mounted on the wall, were faces. Some life-size, others smaller. There were lots of them. Dozens and dozens. They were primal, not crude, clay and soil fired into masks. Eyes just fingers pressed into wet material, mouths carved with wooden spoons (and other tools, scattered across the work tables) captured from the essence of life, personality more than accuracy.

There was talent in their shapes; art making life, not just imitating it. "They really are good," he said, honestly.

"I'm beaming with pride, but I'll bet they're nothing compared to what you do. Or did. Sorry. Hell, I'm not. You may say that you don't anymore, but like I said, I think that when it gets you, it never really lets go, and you can't let go of it."

Can't do it. Can't. It was an exorcism I can't perform, a trick that doesn't work. No way to keep the ghosts away anymore. "It's not that easy. I—I stopped because I couldn't do it." He felt his voice catch.

"I'm sorry to hear that. Really I am. But I'll tell you, just as one 'artistic' type to another, I'll bet you, put good money on it, that what you just need is a change of perspective, a new way of seeing what you do and why you do it."

Waving an arm at the wall, the faces staring back at them: "Like these guys. I dabbled a bit, just using what was lying around. Stuff not doing much of anything, but blowing in the wind." He stooped down, picked up a pickle jar, shook it.

Leaden clouds swirling above larger bits, dark clumps held down by sterner gravity. "But then I started to see more in it. What it could be, not just what it was. Like this one, picked it up in Needles, brought it back here. Just some dust, you know, but then I thought about what it meant to me, how I felt about it, so I stuffed it into a pocket, brought it home with me. It took me a while. Screwed up a lot of them." Pointing to a tiny face, smaller than the others, not as finely crafted: "But after a time, I finally managed to get it."

A wistful expression silhouetted his face that Doud found immeasurably pleasing. He had to fight against entering his heat, his warmth, and kissing him.

"Isn't that what art's about? If you got to, you got to. I realized that when I first started to do these silly things. Now it's why I'm here. I mean, sure, I do all that other stuff people do but now I also look at things and wonder what I can take, change around. It's great. Oh, man, it's like the best kind of drug, the best kind of sex. But there's more to it, you know. It's like I'm changing nothing into something. That's what it's all about, right?"

Doud's vision wavered. Tears, he realized. It had been so long, he almost didn't recognize the giddiness of hope. Far too long.

There was a lot this buff desert sculptor could share with him: art, a man to hold and love, or even just sex, but then the tears eased, stopping even before they could begin.

Vince was human. Doud wasn't.

But they could be the same. All it would take would be a kiss, an intimate exchange of primordial fluids. The kind of kiss that only Doud could give. Lean forward, press lips to lips and then take Vince into himself, draw him up, crumble his body, snap his bones, convert the flesh and blood, and muscle and tissue, into liquid. Then push it backwards, refill Vince's empty sack with changed life, a new liquid essence.

They'd be equals. Artistic, gay, and whatever Doud was. Two men, together, in the desert, making art, making love.

No. No hesitation. No doubt. Never again. He liked Vince, liked him a lot. There was a life, an assurance in Vince, that Doud wanted to lose himself in. He'd lived in the smothering blankets of doubt and shame for so long, the burning passions of Vince were like the sun finally getting to the shade. Liked him, might even come to love him, but they would always be apart. Vince was a gangly desert rat, all tan and muscles, face a lovely dance of bright teeth and brilliant eyes, but he was a man. Doud, no matter how much he tried to act like one, wasn't.

He'd always be alone. There shouldn't be anyone else like him. If he did it, if he reached out to Vince, made him, it would begin all over again, the same thing that always happened. Vince would be altered, yes, but not just into a person like Doud.

But a thing, just like Sergio.

"You're right," Doud said, moving away, putting distance between himself and temptation. "You've made me think." Truth in that: even through his discomfort and sadness Doud was aware of a shift in view, a change in himself by listening, looking at Vince's sculptures, and thinking of his own paintings.

"I'm glad!" Vince said with a bright grin of flawless porcelain. "I always say that thinking is a good thing, but there are times, you know, when it really is better to just switch off the brain and let the body do it all."

"Vince…" he said, ending what he wanted to say with a sigh. "I want to, I really do. But I can't. Maybe later, when I get this all taken care of. But not right now." He glanced away rather than see Vince's forlorn face. "I have to find Sergio. You said you had some idea where he could be. Please, I really do need your help."

"Doud, my man. I—I mean…" He tried again, calmer: "I gotcha. Now I must admit that I…yeah, I was hoping we could get to know each other better, but I'll tell ya, I'm not disappointed. Not at all. You see I've found out a few things about the world and life and all that, being out here where things can move damned fast. Like this rock here, I've learned to take it easy. No rush at all." Face glowing, he brightened with each word. "Besides, I really like you. And for folks that I really like, I'll do all kinds of things, even stick my dick back in my pants. So let's say we get into some air conditioning and go through those magazines I mentioned. I know he's got to be in there somewhere. We'll find him. You'll see. I promise."

"Thank you." The world, or at least Vince's backyard piece of it, seemed brighter, lighter, his personal gravity less demanding, more understanding. "That means a lot to me."

"But I'll tell you, I do have one teeny, tiny request to make of you, Mr. Doud. Nothing big, mind, you. Well, not in that way," Vince said, his laughter nervous but with a tinge of honesty. "Just a little something between two pals who may—who knows?—be more than that someday. Do you mind?"

"Please. You've been a great help."

"Then perhaps you won't mind. Well, I hope you won't. It's just that I could really do with a kiss. Just a sweet, little, friendly kiss. Please?"

*R*UN!
She saw him. He saw her. No question about that. No question at all. Still, she hesitated. In the cool, dusty living room, looking at the door, she couldn't move. Light was behind him, outlining him with a dull yellow afternoon.

Paralysis—until Sergio saw her, and smiled.

Paralysis *lifted*. Movement *granted*. Legs finally obeying her will, she spun around, and began to sprint in the general direction of *away*. But even though she was moving, the air felt like syrup, as if she was at the bottom of a translucent, sluggish sea.

Her breathing was a bellows in her ears. Pushing herself through the thick air, she tried to focus on a steady, simple repetition: Forward, leg up, leg down, push, move forward, leg up, leg down, push, move forward, away from the door, back towards the living room.

She could feel him behind her. The kitchen was on the hazy, indistinct side of a huge expanse, but there was another exit.

Oh shit oh shit oh shit oh shit, was her thoughts, an endless loop in her mind. The kitchen might be too far away, but bright golden daylight was coming through another way out, through the plaster and lath-ringed gap in the wall.

Faster; she tried to/had to move faster. A scream filled her chest, trying to push its way up her throat, but couldn't make it past her gasping inhales and exhales.

Light. Somehow, she wasn't sure how, she'd put one leg down, pushed, and repeated herself through the weighty air until she was *there*, at the hole in the wall.

A second's pause to appraise: it was wide enough, but how far down to the ground was it? The sun was dazzling, making everything blaze painfully, stabbing painfully into her eyes.

Senses magnified in panic, imagination running faster than her legs, she could feel him in the room behind her, running towards her, his mouth stretched, open too wide to be human, just like Doud's hungry, ravenous roar the night before. Her terror knew—*knew*—that he was there, right there, ready to grab her, spin her around, put those awful lips to hers.

Flexing her legs, she propelled herself through the broken wall and out into unknown space. No idea how far up, or what was exactly below, but she did it anyway. Anything was better than what was chasing her.

She flew. Mind racing, heart keeping pace with its racing, she thought, thanks to her stretched, distorted time sense, *got to get the hell away from here,* just before she hit the ground.

Legs hitting first, she slipped, collapsed into a crouch. Pain throbbed up from her thighs and ankles, rushing past even the fear thudding in her ears.

Up onto her feet, pushing away, began running again. Weeds stung her face, her sprint through their thick patches a loud shushing in her ears. Tearing through the thin stalks, her feet slid and skipped over irregularities, ripples and ruts, or half-buried rocks in the fallow field.

Legs pumping, the curtain of dead, yellow stalks parting in front of her, Shelly's mind feverishly mapped *You Are Here* against what she remembered of the town, trying to find the shortest distance between the points of *Here* and *Anywhere But Here.* The house was at the end of a short road, the short road connected with a 't' to an arterial, the arterial to the main road. But all of it was too far away.

Too far away but then a horrible revelation: her mental map was wrong. The house, the roads, the weeds, the dirt and dust were all hemmed in by, bordered by a maze of jingling, chiming—

Shelly was on her back. How did she end up on her back, rocks grinding into her spine, clouds of yellow, powdered dirt swirling in front of her, dead weeds waving back and forth against the too-brilliant yellow sun?

Chain link fence, which she'd run smack into. Crawling to her feet, picking herself up from the dusty earth, she swore at herself, a torrent of coughing profanity. Then, she recalled what the chain link was there for, and *"Fuck"* burst out: a metal cage to keep people out. It also kept her in.

Get back on your feet. Move! But when she did, sudden aches and sharp pains raced up and down her right side, along her ribs, and on the skin covering her cheeks and neck. Bringing her hand up, she stroked her face, felt slickness. Pulling her hand away, she glanced at her palm, her grimy fingers. Saw blood.

"Wait!" came a well-known voice from behind her, back towards the house.

Looking away from her bleeding hand, she saw him sweeping through the dead weeds, sunlight flashing through a few stray strands of long hair.

No thoughts, not enough time for that. Seeing him so close lit a new, hot fire in her already burning lungs. Weeds whipped, rocks and furrows tried to trip her up, but this time she sprinted, not just suspecting, worrying, but rather completely, absolutely knowing that the devil was right at her heels.

A gale came out of nowhere, a hard buffeting of air that rushed past her, kicking up a stinging, billowing cloud. Dandelions, stunted sunflowers and butter-yellow grasses swirled and parted, waved and broke, filling her vision with nothing but tumbling stems, cart-wheeling seeds, fluttering leaves.

"Wait…just wait," Sergio said, panting, his phrasing still musical, still sing-song. In front of her, in the middle of a spontaneously flattened, smashed down clearing, he looked the same as before: black jeans, work boots, long hair tied back by a cheap band. But this time his shirt was as blue as the sky behind him. "Will you please stop?"

"Get the fuck away from me!" she yelled, twisting to run in the opposite direction.

Behind her, he said something, but she couldn't make out what, the moving grass hushing him, obscuring his words. Even if she could have heard, she wouldn't have listened.

The windstorm again, a pocket hurricane. Stones and dirt pelted her face, made her eyes water.

Then he was clutching her shoulder. "Hold it!"

Jerking away, she went to run, but then couldn't. Exhaustion weighed her down, wrapped her in paralysis. The wind, the gale, the small hurricane that had been weaving in and out of the fields…she knew what it was, the knowledge not making her happy. It'd been Sergio, moving too fast for her to see.

Just like Doud, but without a conscience. He could move faster than she could see. For him, she might as well be standing still. Escape wasn't an option. It never had been.

"You're bleeding," he said, with a strange grin on his face, like the sight of her, or gleam of the blood, was somehow very pleasant.

CHAPTER 23

HEART STILL POUNDING IN her chest, Buddy Rich imprisoned somewhere next to a major aorta, still sending frantic escape rhythms through her body, but now not as fast, not quite as panicked. *I'm going to die* came as actually a relief, the responsibility for saving herself long gone against this tall, dark and vicious reality.

"Sorry I don't have something for your face," he said, struggling for breath. "Maybe back in my car."

Same eyes, same nose, same cheeks, same lips, same as before, but his body perhaps a shade more drawn, slightly thinner.

"Well? Come on, get it over with," she said, wiping her bloody mouth with the back of her hand. "I don't like to be kept waiting."

"What?" he said, puzzled. "What are you saying?"

"You know. You know! Well, Doud's not here. Just little ol' me."

"Not here? Shit—" A bit of fear there, and he swiveled, as if that old boyfriend was going to part the weeds and mysteriously reveal himself.

"So you're just going to have to settle for Jewish today." Her bravado shocked her. Might as well go out on your feet. "Slightly fattening, but quite tasty I'm told."

"Look," Sergio said, lips compressed tight. "I have to warn him about something. I can't go into it right now, but you've got to tell me where he is."

"Fuck yourself, asshole." Easy come, quickly gone, her bravery popped like an overfilled balloon, speech crackling with stress: too loud, too sharp. Balance as well as courage lost. Her foot rolled over a stone and she began to topple backwards.

A blur, a gust of wind, and his hand was encircling her arm. "Got you," he said, grinning. "You okay?"

"Yeah, right, sure." She jerked herself free, cautiously retreated, wary of unstable ground. "Warn him, my ass. I know about you. I know what you are. Go fuck yourself, got it? Go. Fuck. Yourself. I'm not saying anything, and I'm sure as shit not going to tell you where he is. So you might as well kill me. Get it over with."

"What are you talking about? I just want to make sure…" He stopped, changed what he wanted to say. "What the hell's going on here?"

"Don't play fucking games with me!" she shrieked. It bounced back as a haunting echo from the house. "Don't jerk me around. He told me about you. I know you're a fucking creep. So get it over already will you? Shit or get off the fucking pot!" An idea: noise. Make enough and someone's bound to notice. People will come. Police will come. Scream as loud as you can.

"Hold it," he said, softly. "Just hold it a minute, okay? Okay? You going to listen? I don't know what he's told you, but all I want to do is give him a message."

Italian. She wished, suddenly, that she knew Italian. Then she'd be able to really understand what the hell he was talking about.

Her guts, though, weren't speaking any language she knew. They were coming to her all garbled and indistinct, not making any kind of sense. Run was what she should be doing, logically speaking, but internally speaking…she didn't. "I'm not getting this. If you're trying to con me, then you might as well give up. I'm not going to tell you where he is. No way. Not happening. Got it? If you want that, you're going to have to go ahead and kill me. Do we understand each other?"

"What? No…just back up a second. I'm just trying to find him—"

Her stomach clenched, cramped. Metaphors flared in her mind: lion ready to leap, cobra pulling back to bite, hawk soaring to strike, psycho-maniac-something-or-other preparing to attack. But he didn't. Instead, he just stood in front of her, jittery and… scared?

He was smaller than she remembered or she'd just inflated him before, making him bigger, badder than he was, after he'd walked into her gallery. What the fuck is going on?

"Aren't you listening? I'm not going to tell you anything. In fact, I'm going to turn around and walk away. Kill me if that's your plan, but I'm not going to tell you where he is."

And she did it. She actually did it. On her heel, a half-spin, and began to walk. Off to the left, above the tops of the yellow stalks was the gray, peaked roof of the house. That's where she'd go, that's where he'd walk.

That's where she tried to walk.

His hand was on her again, and she screamed. The volume and pitch shocked her: the pressure of fury, fear, panic tearing up and out, like a rusty tool scraping up her throat. But it came out loud, and long, and strong.

"God, will you just stop?!" he said, louder but nowhere near as blaring as her cry, his hand staying tight around her upper arm.

His voice, its volume, but also that he spoke, just spoke, and did nothing else, got to her. The pressure dropped, the yell ebbed, dimmed, faded, eased. Just enough remained behind for her to say, "Take your hand off me."

"Calm down. Please." Voice quavering, he went on: "Just take it easy. I don't want to hurt you—" Wrong thing to say, his face said, body agreeing as he fanned fingers in front of his face, trying to erase the words. He tried again: "I'm not going to hurt you, okay? I'm just looking for Doud. I know what you said, I heard you the first time. There's someone I…someone I know. I have to warn Doud to stay away from him. It's very important."

"Don't lie to me. Find another piece of bullshit, 'cause that one just isn't working."

"I'm not lying. I came here looking for my friend, like I said. I told him about this place. I thought he might have come here looking for Doud. That's all."

"I've heard. 1916 or some shit like that. I know the whole story. You and he are…whatever the hell you are, but you're both real old and you have to…feed, right?"

Shock, but not enough to keep him from talking: "He told you? Why?"

"We're not like that. Just friends, okay? Just friends. He blabbed to drag me along, to get me away from you."

"From me? What do you mean? I know he tried to…but that was a long time ago. I don't want to hurt him." That last was soft, almost a murmur.

Oh, fuck. "You weren't after us?"

"No. No, I said that. I came to LA to find him, to warn him. But that's all. I wasn't chasing you."

"Yeah, right, like I'm supposed to believe you didn't leave that thing here for us to find? Your 'message' for Doud?"

"What message? I told you, I just got here."

Her guts spoke, in English this time, or the nearest body equivalent. *He doesn't know.* "There was someone here, one of you, a thing like Doud. A monster, weird and pissed off. Doud said it was a message you'd left for him to find. He killed it. Said it almost killed him."

The emotion on Sergio's face was familiar, one she knew all too well. To see it, all she had to do was look in the nearest mirror. "No…that doesn't make any sense," he said, terrified.

"Why don't you explain it all to me, okay? Start at the damned beginning."

"Doud and I…we knew each other a long time ago."

"Would it help if I said it for you? You two had the hots for each other in 1900 or so, right? But something happened—" Now was her chance, but she couldn't say "He tried to kill you."

"I ran away. I hid, went out to the desert for a while."

"Okay, then you realized you had to kill him before he gets to you again, so you show up at my shop, try to get me to tell you where he is, but I don't give in. You come out here, leave us that hungry little present for us to find. Somehow it gets screwed up, so you're here searching for him. But like I said, I'm not talking."

"No, that's not it. I just want to warn him, that's all. I don't want to hurt him." Each letter was sharp, precise, like he was cutting it into stone, hopefully large enough for even her to see. "There's this man, the friend I mentioned, he's the one who wants to kill him. I came here to try and stop it."

Shit. Shit. Shit. It came down, crashing and banging around her ankles. The illusions she'd built up about what'd been going on tipped, tilted, and fell over: crash, bang, boom. It wasn't that she suspected he was telling the truth, she knew it. "He…Doud's not here. He drove off. He said the monster, that thing back at the house, told him something. That's why he called it a message. Thought you left it, so he went after you. But you didn't leave it, did you? Who was it? Who's trying to kill us?"

Shaking his head: "He doesn't know you. Doud, yeah, he knows about him. That's who he wants. I guess you could say he's my boyfriend. Ex-boyfriend. Vince. His name's Vince."

Her thoughts went *Oh, no, oh, no* then her mind, body, whole self went suddenly quiet, quickly still at her deeper understanding.

Galahad.

THE BAREST TOUCH OF lips, almost a hint.

Their warm breaths mixed, became hot as they got nearer.

Then there was contact. The desert air ignited, burned between them.

Doud was blissfully free of thought except for a freewheeling cloud of images, all of them Vince, all golden naked, in many novel places, many ways. But no real thoughts, none of those: all of them burned off, roasted away from the heat between their lips.

It was a good kiss. A damned good kiss.

It was also an easy kiss, a glide of silken skin, a sharing of breaths.

They enjoyed this dance. After a long, elegant minute, they parted with gentle laughter from both of them.

Then they were together again. An even better kiss, if that was possible.

The first touch of tongue to tongue was shocking, electric, and Doud's spine stiffened, his muscles locked with a surge of sensation. It had been too long. Too many kisses to eat, not enough that'd been a touch, person to person, man to man. This wasn't just good; it was better than good.

They explored each other's mouths, a warm, moist tongue ballet in the middle of a summer day in the desert. It got even hotter, but not because of the weather. In their contact, the world shrank down to just the two of them and the further rising temperature.

Light, uplifted, Doud felt cut free. Pleasure floated him up, soared in his mind. Guilt was gone, shame vanished. He was kissing Vince. Just that, that's all there was, all he was: kissing Vince. Doud kissing Vince.

That cloud became a storm of half-dreams, sensual bursts and surges. Wonders and delights. Textures: the sliding of soft skin, the strength of muscle against muscle, and more. Smells: the salty bite of bodies together, the musk of excitement, and more. Tastes: the hot spice of desire, the dull beating of pleasure in their mouths, and more. All kinds of hopes, one after another, further momentum to his body's rise.

It felt brand new, totally unique. Had it been *that* long? It must have been, for him to forget how wonderful a simple kiss could be. How many years?

Back when iron wheels rattled on cobblestone streets? Back when gas lamps hissed and sputtered, throwing flickering light on pale, ghostly faces? Green glass bottles behind grease-fogged pharmacy windows? Starched collars, like a knife held to your throat? The lazy claps of horses trotting through a city? The moaning hum of prop planes? Planning a day, a week, a month, by a ration book? Radios that were warm, that crackled like stiff paper being wadded up? A long time. A very long time.

Long time brought up a name.

Cold water. Freezing rain. The glow, the burning inside him, went out like a puff of breath across a candlewick. There one moment, gone the next, all because of a name.

Putting his hands on Vince's strong, broad chest, he gently pushed. As he did, he began to close his mouth, break the seal between them.

That's when it became more than just a kiss.

CHAPTER 25

Doud's past cooled him down, his recollection of years before, but also just a few hours ago, dimming the glow, brought him back to earth.

Sergio. Responsibility made his body tense in a different way: it squared his shoulders, made his fingers curl into fists.

As Doud broke away, Sergio was on his mind once again, not from years, or even hours ago, but rather in a much more immediate way.

Vince's kiss was good, great, but also absolutely, positively, not human.

Panic. He fought to force them apart, to break the kiss, but Vince's arms were wrapped too tightly around him, clasped too firmly behind his back. Through his fear, he could feel Vince's strong lips curl into a smirk, never breaking the seal he'd locked them together.

Then it started: the inhalation, the draw. It was a signal, the release of bottomless hunger, the beginning of consumption. But this was Vince's hunger, and Doud was the one being consumed.

Down below (liver and kidney below) Doud's body sharply, wetly broke. Warmth flowed, flooded, rose up and filled his mouth with acid, the thick metallic taste of blood.

Up it went, bubbling around Doud's tongue, and teeth and lips, then out and into Vince.

From his years being on the other end, Doud knew the time-line for the process all too well. He didn't have much time.

Then there were two Douds, side by side. One of them, in Vince's arms, just wanted to let it all happen. No more pain, no more life, no more anything. Nothing to worry about ever again. Knives couldn't do it, guns couldn't do it, even starving himself couldn't do it. But this could: the irony of being food instead of feaster.

All he had to do was…nothing. All he had to do was allow it: be drained, drawn in, depleted. All he had to do was relax, like sleeping, and never wake up again.

But the other Doud, the one who wanted to find out what the fuck was going on, who was angry at being lied to, who was pissed that his little dream of just a kiss, man to man, friend to friend, lover to lover, was a vicious lie, that side won, that side *screamed*.

"*No!*" he yelled into Vince's mouth, sound bubbling up through the surging blood and fluid.

Pressure, and with that bolt of furious emotion, Vince hesitated.

Forcing his arms into a better position, Doud pushed against him as hard as he could, twisting his head away, working against the suction of the kiss.

It worked. The seal broke, ending with a torrent of blood and body juice surging out of Doud's mouth, spraying Vince with a thick hose of body fluids.

"Fuck!" Vince shrieked as the liquid splashed his face, burning his abruptly open, and very wide, eyes. "Fuck!" he repeated, heels of his hands jammed into his sockets, trying to rub away the acids.

Free of the suction, weakness slammed down hard on Doud, leaden exhaustion forcing him to his knees, caps jamming painfully down onto the cement patio.

"Fuck you," Vince howled, pupils still hidden by the heels of his hands. "Fuck you to hell!"

Get up. Doud's breathing was ragged, rasping erratically in and out. The backyard was splashed, smeared and streaked with pools of fluid: water, bile and blood. His water. His bile. His blood. Not a lot, but enough to make his head swim, his flesh weak. *Got to get up. Got to get out of here.*

"Shit," Vince said, voice showing his own shock was starting to ebb.

Get up! This time his body began to listen to what his thoughts were yelling. Glancing up from the Rorschach splats of his life, he saw Vince a dozen or so feet away, back at the sliding glass door, blinking furiously. His shirt and jeans were pink from Doud's inner fluids, still glistening in the afternoon light.

Crawling to his feet, steadying himself with a palsied grip to one of Vince's workbenches, he chanced a look at his hand, pale and shrunken, bones obvious against wrinkled skin. Old…like an old man's hand, a mummy ready for the museum. A corpse waiting for a grave. Beyond his hand was the table. On it were the tools of Vince's craft. Above the tools were the faces, a wandering parade of primitive sculptures. Below the table, he couldn't see but rather *knew*, about the jars.

So obvious. Jars of dust, the raw materials of his craft, the capturing in clay the remains of the once living. *Why didn't I see it before?*

I didn't want to.

CHAPTER 26

"WHAT AN IDIOT. WHAT a fucking idiot."

Doud swung away from the jars and the faces. Vince, face streaked, paler where he'd scraped and rubbed the burning fluids away, was clearly suppressing a laugh.

"I mean…*shit!*" Then it came out, finally, rough and strong. "What a fucking moron. What a fucking let-down."

Pushing against the edge of the table, Doud locked his knees, trying to stand as smoothly as possible but failed, though, when his legs gave out in a sudden surge of weakness. He didn't fall, but he did stagger, eventually righting himself.

"Stupid fucker." Vince sneered, flexing his shoulders, releasing some kind of long-stored tension. "Christ. To think that I was worried about you."

Mind a fog of exhaustion and confusion, Doud fought to puzzle out what the hell Vince was saying, but nothing materialized. Instead, he concentrated on simply not collapsing.

Vince took a step, then another. Close enough to touch him, Doud smelled the bitter acid of hot blood all over him.

"I can't believe it. You, the big, bad Doud? What a crock of shit."

Clarity came painfully. Belly groaning in hunger, his chest a hollow drum, his skin papery, Doud knew he'd come close to having his liquid life sucked out of him. Come close to dying.

He wanted to shout it all away, release his agony, the hunger that hammered at the front of his mind, but most of all what Vince was saying in a roar of frustration. He also wanted to run, as fast and as far as he could.

"W-What do you mean?" he managed to croak, throat raw and burning.

"Like I said," Vince yelled up at the sky, as if seeking confirmation from above that he was right. "Stupid. How you've managed to stay alive all these years, I'll never know."

Doud didn't respond, just kept inhaling and exhaling.

"I know all about you, courtesy of your 'friend' Sergio. And, yes, he did this to me," he said, brushing his tanned, coarse hands down his chest, his filthy shirt, referring to his body and what had been done to it.

Vince stepped forward again, so twisted around to look back, scoping for a way out, but saw only brilliant white sunlight, the shade cast by the roof above, far beyond, the yellow stone rise of the boulder, and still farther beyond the shimmering metal of a chain-link fence.

"What a pure, grade-A fucker you are. Bad enough you tried to kill him, but then you have to sit in the back of his brain to almost drive him nuts. 'Doud did this,' 'Doud did that.' Every goddamned day, the same goddamned thing: 'Doud, Doud, Doud.' I got so fucking sick of hearing about you."

Suddenly there was hot sunlight in Doud's eyes. Without being aware of it, he'd stepped back, out of the shade. He could feel his body drying out even more.

"I told him this place wasn't big enough for me, him, and the big bad motherfucker that started all this. You should have seen him," he laughed again, an echo of his fundamental sound. A satisfied bass rumble. "You should have seen his face when I said we should kill you. Put a fucking stake in your heart."

The sun was beating him, cooking him, boiling more and more of him away. He couldn't stop moving backwards, though, he had to keep putting distance between them.

"'Oh, Doud, my love, my sweetness, come and kiss me,'" Vince's mouth opened too wide, became a swallowing abyss, a fleshy maw. But then he shrank it back, inch by inch, to be able speak. "What a fucking moron. I've been following your ass since Barstow, after leaving you that 'present' at your old place. Thanks, by the way; you saved me from trucking out to fucking LA. You never saw me, never figured any of it out—but then you never really figured any of it out, did you? Not in two hundred damned years. He told me about you always beating your breast: 'Poor me, poor hungry, me.' So stupid: all that pointless, useless guilt. He tried to give me the same shit, but I didn't buy it."

A sound like a wind chime ringing, Doud realized he'd backed all the way up against the chain link that stretched from the border of the house to the edge of the rock.

"Face it, Doud: everyone eats. We just happen to eat everyone."

The sun was scorching, relentlessly burning, baking him, drying Doud. Being in it for the last minute or so had started his belly growling again, had woken the emptiness deep down.

Images flickered across Doud's mind, fueled by his fury, projected onto the inside of his skull: reaching out, grabbing Vince by the neck, bringing him close, putting his lips to Doud's lips. Then the suction, and Doud feasting on his moisture, his blood and life. He'd pull him in, swallow him down, listen to his bones creak, crack, break; watch as his eyes shrank, wrinkled, then get pulled back into his shrinking skull.

No. Not yet. He'd already made one humiliating mistake, he couldn't afford another.

Doud was weak, nearly depleted. If he attacked, he'd run dry. If he ran dry, he'd no longer be in control. No longer in control, he'd become a desperate, starving animal. Starving animals were not smart, not clever. They couldn't plan. If he couldn't plan, he'd lose. It was as simple as that.

Anger ebbing, it was replaced by fact, by cold reason. Vince was too strong, Doud was too empty. His only chance was to run.

Which was clearly what Vince wanted: "Are you ready, great and powerful Doud? All set to break with tradition, ready to be the meal this time? I hope so, because I'm all itchin' for my favorite game: playing with my food."

CHAPTER 27

S ERGIO'S CAR WAS A bright little toy, an immaculate candy-red finish topped by a pure white dab of canvas: an Italian powerhouse of an automobile, probably costing more than everything Shelly owned, had ever owned, put together.

It made her very happy, though, to realize that she had something Sergio would give anything, even his precious Ferrari, for.

After her hefty dose of panic, being able to wear a self-satisfied grin felt wonderful. It was a just a few words ("Come to Needles") but the fact that she knew it, and Sergio didn't, meant she had some degree of control over what was going on.

It had taken her a very long, very confused minute to compose herself after Sergio had uttered his own, singular, magic word. A black magic word, actually, since it had made her knees go liquid.

Vince.

They'd only been together for a few minutes, and by all rights, she shouldn't have even remembered how she'd gotten from Doud's house to the hotel, let alone the name of the man who'd driven her, or her sarcastic nickname for him. But she did. Vince: tanned, buff, good teeth, a hick's affect without the inbreeding.

Had she known? From what Sergio implied, she'd driven with more than one immortal predator in the last few days. Had some kind of new radar kept his name and face in her mind, unconsciously recognizing him as a member of Doud's horrible family tree? Had she developed her own twisted form of gaydar, except instead of fags she'd tuned in to a different, scarier frequency?

"I have to find him," Sergio'd said before they stepped out of the weeds, before she'd seen his car in the drive.

"Yeah, well join the crowd," she'd snapped, running her fingers through her hair, wincing at the tugs of knots. "We'd better get going."

"No way. You're going to stay here, where it's safe." Craning his neck, he'd looked around for a way out of the backyard.

"Fuck that. You don't even know where to go. I do. I'm going with you." Weeds snapped against the edge of her hand as she chopped a path. A burr snagged a finger and a flash of pain brought the torn skin to her mouth. She tasted dirt, sweat, and a hint of blood. Remembering her face, she stroked it, feeling a few brittle scabs.

"It's too dangerous," he stage-whispered, lost, it seemed, in his own mind as well as the field.

"Hey, I'm not arguing that. But I have to go. I know more than you do, even if it's just from Doud's side. You want that, right?"

Blinking a few times, he'd said, "Yes, I do, but no, it's not going to happen. Vince can get pretty angry. You can't be anywhere near him."

"Then you need all the help you can get. By the way, the house and your car are that way." She'd pointed towards the ashen gray peak of the house, a sliver of gray triangle peering above the stalks. "I know where Doud's gone, thanks to your boyfriend's little message. So I'm going with you, or you'll never know where to find him."

She was ready, tensed up and prepared to continue arguing, threatening, blackmailing, whatever it took to get in that car and go with him.

Why?

Back at the hotel, she'd felt small, lost, alone: just another face in a very human crowd. Without Doud, she was just a middle-aged woman running a failing gallery. That wasn't life; it was existing. That was why she'd gone back to the house, to try and understand him, but in no small way to also keep the excitement of Doud and his horrible, yet fascinating, life around her.

That was then, but as she'd walked through the crackling weeds, she realized there was more to it.

Much, much more.

What it was, wasn't quite clear yet. She couldn't see what it was, a mental fog hid it, obscured it from her mind, but whatever this hidden reason was, she knew she had to go with Sergio. She had to see Doud again. She had to see it through.

Even if it meant getting killed.

CHAPTER 28

Afinal curtain of weeds parted and there was the house, the dirt road, and Sergio's Italian toy. In dusty quiet, they walked towards it. No arguing, no blackmail, no more threats.

Unlocking the driver's side door, he leaned in, pushed a switch and let her in. The interior was burning hot, and even though she didn't want to, she hissed in discomfort as she sat down.

"Okay," he said, staring out the windshield. "You're coming. But when I tell you to get out, you get out. Got it?" Drumming his long fingers on the wheel, he tap-tap-tapped, pale skin a harsh contrast against black leather. "He told you about us, what we are, right?" he said, refusing to look at her directly.

"Some stuff. Just the basics. You and he had a thing back in the silent picture days. That something happened between you two. He isn't exactly a fountain of info, you know."

"I know. I guess he hasn't changed. What else did he say about me? Us, I mean."

"Not a lot." *Wish I had a cigarette.* In Doud's car, she knew when she could bend or break the rules and when she didn't dare. But this road was unfamiliar, the guy behind the wheel very different. She dug out her make-up mirror and a wad of tissue, checked herself out in the reflection. The scabs were small, just dirty commas on her cheek and forehead. Grateful they weren't larger punctuations, she set about cleaning herself up as much as she could. "Hadn't we better get going? God knows what your crazy boyfriend could be up to by now."

"He tried to kill me, you know," Sergio suddenly said, voice very soft.

Tissue and mirror back in, she snapped her purse shut. "Which one?" she said, trying to laugh the tension off.

He turned dusky eyes to her. "Doud." Sigh. "I ran away, thought he was going to come after me."

"He said something about that." *I'm sorry* wanting to come out. No clue, though, as to why, or why she didn't let it.

"I left town. He told me what I'd become, but it was frightening to be on my own. I didn't know what to do, so I sort of made it up as I went along."

The car was getting hot. Sweat began to bead on her upper lip. When she wiped it away with the side of her hand, salt in perspiration met the cut on her finger and she winced at the stab of unexpected pain.

Sergio's stare returned to the dash. All of a sudden, he started the engine, awakening a growling, high-octane beast. Instantly the air conditioning whirred up, and the hot interior began to cool. "I went to him for help but he tried to kill me."

Perspiration, and so the pain from her finger gone, she felt focused and sharp, like each of his syllables were spoken with the ringing of a crystal bell, whether she wanted to hear it or not.

"There was this assistant director on a picture I was working on. Jeffrey Namti. Greasy little thing. Someone told him too many times he was cute, but he was just precious. High-strung, too. Liked to be on top of everything. If you said anything, every other word had better be 'Jeffrey' or he got pissed-off. He found out that Doud and I were together. Doud had just…made me.

But Namti didn't know that. He just saw that we had something he didn't. I was in the studio, cleaning up, when he came in."

One hand on the gearshift, he slipped it back, and to the right, with a fluid, practiced motion. "I didn't know what he wanted. All I know is, I got scared, and…he told you, right? What we do? I killed Namti. I thought he was going to hurt me."

The motor changed the pitch of its growl and they reversed away from the house. "I saw Doud the next day. He…that's when he tried to kill me."

They'd gone back far enough. Another quick slap of the knob (forward, to the left) and they pulled forward. "I ran. I got out of Hollywood, and went back east. I didn't know really what else to do. I thought he was chasing me. I thought I saw him in Minneapolis, in Chicago, in Boston, in New York. I went to London for a while, but I thought I saw him in Hyde Park feeding the pigeons. A couple of years after that, I didn't see him anymore. I guess you can get used to anything, even the idea that someone is trying to kill you."

Cranking the wheel, he pointed the car down the road. Shelly didn't feel the road at all: no ruts, or rocks, ever see the distant asphalt ribbon of the highway, or even the too-blue sky overhead. Instead, she was lost in imagining his life, of being lost and alone in a foreign city, hearing the chatter and grumble of alien languages. Then, on top of that, what little she remembered from school and the History Channel: Hitler, concentration camps, bombings, tanks, refugees, burning cities, Paris with jackboots, Prague and the Jews, corpses in streets, but through it all—a certain face, a certain pair of eyes, that could be anywhere. Doud's face, Doud's eyes.

Pressing her thumb and forefinger to the top of her nose, she tried to massage away the onslaught. There was no reason his reminiscences should have had such a strong impact on her.

Except what he said sounded way too sincere, too true, and all too frightening.

"After the war I came back. Got tired of it, I guess. Being frightened all the time, I mean. Always on the run." He paused, rolling something around in his mind. "I wanted to go home."

"I can relate," she said, instantly wincing. *How the hell can I?*

"I doubt it. No insult." They'd glided up to a stoplight. "It wasn't a bright thing to do, but I did it anyway. By then, I'd guessed that he wasn't coming, that maybe even he'd forgotten about me."

"Nope, definitely not that," she said, twiddling with one of the dash vents until it blew cold air into her face.

The light changed and they roared forward. "So what did he say about me? I know you said he was scared I was coming after him."

"You could say that. 'Panicked' more like. He just grabbed me and—*zoom!*—we were getting the fuck out of Dodge. Dragged me all the way here because it was supposed to be safe. So much for that plan, eh? So who left that creep back at the house? Your pal, Vince?"

Sergio nodded. "I think so. I went to LA, he went to Barstow, probably to leave that thing. He likes games." Squirming in his seat, he glanced over at her, then went back to looking out at the road. "So, you've known Doud a long time?"

"Long enough, I guess. Dinner and movie kind of thing. Just friends, you know. Met him through the gallery. But you figured that out, right?"

He nodded. "I try to keep track of him. You can imagine why. I'd heard he was back in town six or so years ago. Probably why I started to talk about him to Vince. Stupid. Should have kept my mouth shut."

"Look, about Vince…what the hell's going on here, anyway? Doud said he didn't think anyone else could make any more, but somebody made your boyfriend and that weirdo back at the house. You'd better tell me what the hell's going on, or I'm not going to tell you the secret."

"Secret?"

"Yeah, where Doud went, remember? The little message that thing told him. Where we're supposed to be going? By the way, you want to get on the freeway."

"Right. Right," he said, pointing the machine down a busy street. He was quiet for a few long blocks, then: "I met Vince about ten or so years ago. I was just looking for a boyfriend. It wasn't until later that I thought about trying to change him."

Snorting: "My mom always says you can't change anyone, and if you could, you shouldn't."

"Your mother's a smart woman."

"When she isn't crocked. So you and this Vince guy had a thing going, right? One thing lead to another and you have…well, 'another,' right? How many more of you guys are out there?"

"I've looked, but haven't found anyone else. I really think we're it. Thank god."

"Yeah, it's bad enough that your crazy boyfriend tried to kill us. Don't want it any worse, do we?"

"Was Doud upset? About you coming back?"

"Yeah, I'd consider him upset. Not that you can really blame him. As far as he knows, you're bugfuck crazy."

Blasting up the ramp, the car's engine bellowed with the roar of Italian racing horses.

Soon the scenery was whipping by too fast to see well. Reaching up, she wrapped her hand around her shoulder strap, gripping it tightly.

"Damn," he said, lifting his foot from the gas, easing them down to slightly over the posted limit. "I'm sorry."

"Don't worry about it. We have to get there, right? The faster the better. Not that really, really fast would be better."

Wearing a wry grin, obviously trying to lighten the abruptly leaden atmosphere, he went on: "After I changed him, Vince started acting…well, kind of bugfuck. He liked it too much, you know? I kept trying to help him, show him what Doud'd shown me. But I guess he always kind of believed he was in Doud's shadow, Doud being my first…*the* first and all. A month or so ago, he got really pissed off. Said there wasn't room for all of us, that he didn't want Doud telling us what we could and couldn't do." He was quiet for a minute, looking out at flat, featureless desert plains.

"I never really thought of Doud as being the fatherly type," Shelly said, fumbling with her cigarettes and lighter. *Come on, get the hint.* "But I guess he could be for you guys."

Nodding, he went on. "He said he'd take care of Doud. 'Put him out of our misery,' he said. That's why I went down to LA, to try and find him, and Doud. To warn him."

"Hey, how the hell did Vince know about Barstow, any-way? Doud said it was his special little hideaway, that he kept it a secret."

"He told me, long time ago, probably forgot. I must have told Vince, too. Funny the stuff you tell someone when you think you love them."

"Yeah, I know that way too well," she said, but her tones were dull, hollow. She didn't know. Had no idea about that. "Um, right, this is the way to go."

"I know. I have a good idea of where he went. Vince likes to…work in his studio. That's probably where he tricked Doud into going. Sorry, I needed to find out what was going on."

"Shit, well thanks for telling me. I hope I was helpful," she said, cold with sarcasm.

"I said I was sorry. I meant it. I didn't know what was between you two, what Doud was up to, what he was feeling…all that. It's important."

"I'm sure it was but you could have just fucking asked me, you know? I'm not getting out of the car, you realize. Just keep driving. I'm in this all the way."

"Not happening. Like I said, Vince is pissed off. I don't know what he's going to do, what's going to happen. Anyway, I think Doud would be very upset if anything happened to you."

"I can take care of myself, *thankyouverymuch*. I'm a big girl and I know what the hell's going on, probably more than you do. Just keep driving. Besides, you fuck with me and I'll put in a call to the cops, tell them you're running a crack lab, a bunch of terrorists or something."

His laughter out-roared the Ferrari's engine. "Okay, okay. Truce." He shifted up, changed lanes. "Besides, you can tell me a bit more about Doud, what he's been up to. Why aren't his pictures in your gallery anymore?"

"He took them. Came in and told me he didn't want me to sell them. Later he told me he couldn't paint anymore. That's it. Still, after he told me what he'd been painting with, I could see why he wouldn't want them hanging in someone's foyer. It'd be like putting up an *I'm a bloodsucking creature! Arrest me!* sign. Kind of like him, though: all or nothing. The man lives for absolutes."

"Yeah, that's him alright. I've been thinking about that. I wonder what he wants. What he really wants."

"Got me. I thought he was just a nice little guy, but then he outed himself. Now I don't know what the hell is going on."

"Well, you know more than I do. You're here with me now, going to try and save him. You can't tell me you're just doing this because he's someone who's nice to you. Would you be doing this for someone who's just a friend?"

"I told you, we're pals, okay? I mean he's a good friend—" she cut herself off. Why *had* she come along? Without him, she was just plain-ol'-ordinary Shelly, but with him, she was more than that. Doud was a door to something different, something strange, something very special. Envy. That was part of it. Jealousy that Doud was anything but an old, ordinary, and excruciatingly dull human.

But there was something else, something even beyond his inhumanity. A something she wanted more than anything else.

It was something she'd seen in him, saw on his face, when he talked about Sergio. Disappoint, yeah, fear, sure, but another quality. The same quality she'd just seen lit in Sergio's dark features.

"You still love him, don't you?" she asked him.

Those features swinging towards her, she had a perfect view of his shocked expression. Foot lifting briefly from the pedal, they coasted.

Then turned back. His earth-shaded pupils returned to the impossibly long stretch of asphalt in front of them, looking back out at where it narrowed to an unreachable vanishing point, and without a word he sent the car roaring toward it.

CHAPTER 29

Hᴇ ᴡᴀs ʀᴜɴɴɪɴɢ. Tʜᴇ sun was hot, high, and strong, and Doud was running half as fast as he could. The air was still just air, not syrup. At this speed, friction didn't burn. Materials and surfaces were still firm and solid, not liquid, slippery, or fragile. His vision was crisp, not shifted towards red.

If he wanted to, he could, of course, move that much faster, burn what little fuel sloshed around the bottom of his belly, but it would be a sprint, a one-shot burst of acceleration, using everything up in a few dozen faster-than-the-eye-could-see steps. That was do-able, but afterwards it wouldn't be Doud who was in control.

It would be his hunger.

He couldn't run forever, but he still pushed himself, fueling himself with fear rather than liquid. No idea how long he'd run, or how far back Vince was. Surfacing from the Zen of running, he looked back. Nothing but flat yellow, a dirty gold plain and the fist that was the rock. Vince's house was hidden behind it, not even the fence was visible. That was all. No sign of the house's owner.

Spinning stories, terror put Vince walking around the rock, mouth yawning. Vince waiting for him when he turned around, holding him tight, drinking him like a thirsty man downing a glass of cool, refreshing water.

But, after a few calming breaths, he realized there wasn't any truth to his fears. He was alone; there was nothing but desert and the rock all around him. Then, looking away from the rock, and the house, he looked harder and, for a second, imagined that desert had somehow broken, shifted up: a vertical shape where there had been nothing but horizontal before.

It was a wall. Not high, and made of butter-yellow bricks, the same color as the desert rock. The sun was directly overhead so it barely cast a shadow, making it nothing but a thin razor's slash of darkness on an otherwise hot, gold plain.

It wasn't a high wall. After more running through the baking day, Doud was just tall enough to reach up, touch his fingertips to the top of it.

Then, he thought he heard something, a sound like the wind, but maybe also like a man running fast enough to make a noise *like* the wind. A story? A lie? His terror? Not staying to ponder, he jumped, caught the top of the wall in his dried, paper-crisp fingertips. Even though he didn't have much strength left, he still managed to grip and pull with his straining arms, pushing himself up to the top with his weakened legs.

On the other side was a backyard. More walls to the right and left. It was part of a row of tract homes, tile-roofed, Spanish style, one after another: the end of a sub-division, or the far extension of a suburb.

The yard was empty except for a plastic tricycle dull with dirt and dried mud, cracked where once new, tipped over and discarded where once prized; and a redwood picnic table, newer than anything else, maybe the hope for family get-togethers under the endlessly blue sky.

Doud dropped, disturbing the backyard soil, sending up a lazy cloud of dust. He didn't pause. He knew it wasn't a lie, not a story told by his fears: he knew Vince was somewhere close behind.

But much nearer was something almost as bad. Joining the chorus of aches he'd picked up since beginning his run, his belly rumbled. Hunger pangs.

Either he satiated himself, and soon, or he would lose consciousness, and become a starving pit that would tear through the subdivision until it came across someone, anyone, who was warm, wet, and living.

Right then, as if on cue, a woman stepped out of the house.

CHAPTER 30

Like the plastic tricycle, she'd been new and fresh once, but was now just used and dirty. Her frock was a simple blue housedress. Like the picnic table, though, there was hope for her: her dirty blond hair was at least in curlers.

None of that mattered to Doud. All that was important was that she was alive.

Having just enough bloody fuel, he blurred with speed, and crossed the distance between them in the time it took her to open her mouth, for her to scream.

A flash, a bolt of dirty, wild hair, furtive, wild eyes, and an open mouth, and she was in his arms. The buffeting wind of his acceleration flapped and cracked her dress like a flag.

It was horrible for her and horrible for him. Horrible for her because of his assault, horrible for Doud because he was aware of what he was doing. This wasn't Frank innocently pissing behind a shed, a victim of his mindless hunger.

Doud kissed her, clamping his lips to hers, swallowing her unspoken scream, taking it into himself. Then, an instant later, he took more. Much more.

The warm, wet, fluid life in her boiled from his powerful vacuum, then was sucked up through her chest, until it splashed, and surged into his mouth and down into his belly. Thrashing in panic, her body reeked of the bitter, salty perspiration of her hysteria.

Then the aroma of her fear faded, and her sweat vanished, as it too was drawn back in by the strength of Doud's suction. A dribbling crackle like water poured on a tight drum signaled her internal organs breaking down, every drop of their moisture pulled out.

From tired middle age, her skin became tighter and firmer, and for a second, she looked young again. But the illusion was fleeting. The wrinkles returning, then folding over and over again as more of her body jelled, collapsed, shrunk, liquefied and then was swallowed into Doud.

All in a blink, but Doud never did, not once. He desperately wanted to shut his eyes, but he fought the urge, instead forcing himself to look, as a way of testifying to her death, his murdering of her.

She watched as well, but not for long. Clear at first, her pupils quickly bloomed with cataracts, then ripples formed in the hardboiled whites. From ripples to ridges, from ridges to folds, from folds to collapsing, sucked back into her skull.

Arms and legs withdrawing into the cavity that had once been her torso, they followed her melted heart, lungs, liver, kidneys, going up her convulsing throat, in her withering mouth, and into Doud.

In a few hideous convulsions, the last of her connective tissue dissolved from the suction, and her liquid weight was completely gone. Skin sloughing, the last of her totally broken down, until her remains were nothing but a few pounds of dried tissue that hissed through his fingers, poured onto the ground to form a cone of lifeless powder, grit and minerals at his feet,

Then there was nothing left of her but an empty housedress, and a few streamers of hair that began to twist and roll away in a lethargic breeze.

Gone, she was an easier burden to carry, at least physically. Her dress…he was holding her dress. Letting it go, it fell through his hands with a hush of fabric.

It was a neat and simple way of killing someone. It left nothing behind but dust and powder, hairs and tiny fragments of bone, finger and toenails, fillings sometimes. The wind would scatter whatever was left, or if he had the time, he'd simply brush it away. Nothing would be left but blood in Doud's belly, and guilt in his soul.

I'm sorry. I'm so sorry.

Shame changed, then becoming fury. All his fears, all he'd fought to prevent, had a name: *Vince.* Not because the man was behind him, but instead because of what Doud had seen in the cool shade of that house: faces sculpted out of more dust, the lives Vince had taken only to capture in clay. They'd meant nothing to him, just a source of materials: a stride he'd liked, a face he'd seen as handsome, a style he'd wanted to capture.

He kills to create. I create to remind myself that I kill.

"Well, well," came a too-well-known voice from behind and above. "Would you look at that."

Doud swung. Standing on the wall, hands on his hips, smirk on his tanned face, was Vince.

"A switch hitter." A nod to the powder at his feet. "Bet it makes it easy to find a date on a Saturday night, huh?"

CHAPTER 31

Doud ran, but this time he wasn't empty, wasn't starving. This time he was full, and furious. This time air was syrup, and burned through friction. This time, materials and surfaces weren't firm and solid, but instead were liquid, slippery, and fragile. This time his vision was blurred, shifted towards the red end of the spectrum.

Vince had jumped down from the wall, assuming a *fuck you* pose, after he'd landed and stood up straight. But as Doud had begun to move, Vince had slowed until he was nothing but a cocky statue.

He didn't have much time. If he could catch Vince off guard, he might have a chance.

Putting an elbow out, Doud rushed towards him. At his speed he was a bullet, and would smash into, and hopefully right through, Vince. Fight over, Doud winning. If, that is, Vince didn't see it coming.

Vince did. As Doud closed the gap between them, Vince's body unfroze, his movements going from glacial to natural as he accelerated to match their velocities, rushing to meet Doud head-on.

As their distances closed, Doud saw that Vince had managed to twist his body, turning himself just enough to deflect most of Doud's impact.

Damn, Doud thought as his elbow grazed Vince's chest.

Passing, Vince swung up with his right, right into Doud's chest. Even though he saw it coming, Doud had no time to do anything about it.

A broken rib, even at air-tearing velocities, has a distinct flavor. Doud's mind was instantly full, completely overwhelmed by the hammering ache, a crushing wave of pain.

Luck: Doud managed to stay balanced on his feet as he slid along the ground. Fear gripped his heart across the top of his brain. If they hadn't been going at the same rate, if Vince had been moving a bit faster, if Doud had been moving just a little slower, then Doud's bones would have been bread sticks. Vince would have torn him apart, scattering Doud's pulverized organs in an arc of red, purple, and bits of crumbling bone.

Vince, though, hadn't been distracted by a horrible fantasy of what might have been. He had recovered, spun around, and was heading back towards Doud.

It all became a matter of simple physics. Even with their velocities matched, Vince would hit hard. Hard enough, and Doud would have to slow down. Slowing down would mean their velocities weren't matching. Their velocities not matching would mean Doud's blood, bone, and organs spraying across the hot emptiness of the yard wouldn't be just be a morbid fantasy.

He'd tried to fight, but Vince was still too strong, too focused. In desperation, a solution came to mind. Sacrifice. If he ran even faster, pushed himself to his absolute limit, he might win. He could completely burst with velocity, smash into Vince like a cannon shell, not just a bullet.

But there was a problem. Even if he did it, and pulverized Vince into a *mutual* shower of bone and blood, it wouldn't be over. There was still someone else out there that Doud had to kill. The one who'd created a monster just to deliver a message, a man who'd killed his dreams of eternity, if only a Hollywood one.

Doud swung around. Fight was over. Time for flight. Too fast, and he'd burn, ignite, enflame. Become a charred meteor. Too slow and he wouldn't clear the top, he'd fall right back into Vince's arms.

He'd done it once before, the trick he was about to try, and paid the price with two broken legs, burns, and a cracked pelvis. But he didn't have a choice. He had to get away, think, regroup. First Vince, then Sergio. That would take planning.

Doud ran. Cheeks, nose, forehead, lips, eyes, his face felt like it was being pushed into a fire, flames licking the salt from his face. One kind of burning, the first degree, passed by in an instant. He was well into the second.

If he made it, he'd be depleted, used up. But not empty and, most importantly, away from Vince. Right then, that was all that mattered.

Moving still faster, the skin on the back of his hands bubbling then charring, his clothes crisping from the heat, he felt the moment come.

A sudden memory of explosions, shrapnel, mud, hot copper in the air from blood on the ground, the bite of cordite in his nose. Realizing that every face he saw, every name he heard, may not be there the next day, the next hour, the next minute, stolen by a shot, or the scream of a shell.

There'd been voices. Russian ones close up, German ones carried by the wind from off in the distance. He'd tried to stay as far away as he could, but the war had finally caught up with him in that small village near Urdeska.

Russian. Years later, he couldn't hear the language without thinking of that village, and that night. Off in the distant hills that morning, the battle had finally come to town just before dusk. German soldiers everywhere. The clatter of machine gun fire in the woods, long after the town was theirs. Too little food. Too many prisoners. A very German, very efficient, solution.

He'd been hiding in a barn, then a soldier had come in, no more than a boy a dirty, gray uniform. Up the ladder he'd come, face somehow still cherubic from the lights of burning homes.

Both of them had been hungry and frightened, but Doud had something the boy didn't. Quickening, he'd used up the last of his bloody fuel to rush him, grab him, suck him dry. Soon, the orange flames were gone, revealing an empty gray uniform in Doud's arms, powder mixing with straw.

But the soldier had a friend. A friend with a machine gun. Running wouldn't have worked, as a simple squeeze of the trigger would fill the air with bullets moving faster than Doud ever could. So he did then what he was hoping to do now.

Doud jumped.

Pushing off he began an arc, the beginning of a curve with one end in the yard, the other, hopefully…*away.*

Acceleration, trajectory, inertia, all in the right amount. He'd clear the top. Behind him, Vince would be hopefully unsure, and unable to imitate.

Soaring upwards, smoke from his burning body mixing with the desert air, his vision began to fog, his corneas beginning to scorch. Much more and he'd be blind. Blind, even if he got over the wall, and, he'd be dead.

Pain everywhere, especially on his face, his hands, but with it all a strange kind of joy. The wall was passing below him.

Vince behind, the desert ahead. Precious time bought. If he could survive landing on the other side and not burn up, it would mean time. Time meant a chance at winning. Arcing through the air, he prayed his luck would hold long enough to kill Vince, and then as soon as he could a final kiss, long deserved, to the one who'd started all this.

A late, but necessary, kiss for Sergio.

CHAPTER 32

S HE GAVE UP TRYING to re-engage the Italian. After she'd opened her mouth, saying what she knew was the obvious, Sergio hadn't said a word.

Not that conversation would have been easy. Sergio may not have been in a chatty mood, but his driving spoke way too loudly. The Ferrari's interior was filled with a throbbing mechanical din, as he kept the pedal flat to the floor.

Slumped in her seat, still unsure of the rules, Shelly opened her purse, fondling her gold-plated Zippo, reading and rereading the surgeon general's warning on her pack of cigarettes.

Then she pulled out a single cigarette. Inspecting the unfiltered end, she meticulously pulled a strand of tobacco out and rolled it into a tiny, ragged ball, and kept rolling until it was so small it vanished between her fingertips.

Holding it like a dart, practicing European flair (after all, she was riding in a Ferrari) she retrieved the lighter again and flipped the gleaming top back.

"Please don't," he said, grumbling over the engine's roar. "I hate the smell."

After surrendering, hands up, lighter in one hand, cigarette (still held like a European) in the other, the items went back into the bag, crammed with dramatic flair. "Where we're going—" she began.

Turning, he glanced at her briefly before going back to the dizzying view ahead.

"—what do you think's going to happen? I mean, what's at the end of the road?" She gestured forward.

"I don't know."

"Well, what do you *want* to find there?"

"Haven't thought it out. Not really."

"Then I'll start. You know what I want?"

Nothing but the engine, the sound of air rushing around the windshield, the moan of tires on asphalt.

"I don't know, either," she said to his profile. "Haven't the faintest. I thought I knew, but now I'm not sure. I even had a list, a little from column A, a little from column B. Get out of this alive, have everything be okay with Doud, kill you—"

"Really?"

"I told you about that. Hell, part of me still isn't totally convinced. But that was column A. Column B is hazier. It bothers me, some of the stuff on that list. It really does." Bag tight to her chest, she gazed out the window. "It's like everything around me has changed, or I have. I don't know. When Doud left me back there, it was a relief, but it was also like…something was gone. One thing on that list…I know I shouldn't want it, but I do anyway. You know what I mean?"

"I think I might."

A few more silent miles, then she said, "Yeah, you might. You might." Then she went back to watching the world, the old world, pass them by.

Their destination, it seemed, was closer than she realized. But time, as measured by her wandering mind, was probably not to be trusted. She'd been too busy aimlessly cruising around inside her own head to have a good idea of how long they'd really been driving.

Leaving the road, pulling up and stopping in front of a brick and steel house, her mental haze dissipated. "Nice place," she said as she got out of the car.

"It used to be," he said, with obvious honesty, climbing out with her.

No obvious signs of life. "Do you know they're here?"

"No, but this is the only place I could think of going. If they aren't here, I don't know where they could be." Gesturing toward the road, he added, "Desert that way. Nothing for miles and miles. The town that way," he said, pointing towards a huge rock behind the house.

"Come on, fill me in. What's going on? Doud, I know, at least a little bit, but I don't know anything about your ex-boyfriend."

"I don't know what he's up to. He just told me he was going to kill Doud. That's why I went to LA, then over to Barstow. The rest of it…" He shook his head.

"Fuck, I wish I had a gun. Not that I'd know how to use it. Just would make me feel better." Making a thumb and forefinger pistol, she pointed it off at the horizon, squeezed off a shot.

"Wouldn't do you any good. Not unless you were damned lucky. Doud told me he'd been shot a couple of times. Always managed to pull through."

"He didn't tell me that." Some things you only tell boyfriends, I guess. "So what do we do?"

"Find them first. Figure out what's going on. See if Doud's okay. Can't plan anything until we know what's happened. But if you see Vince, even from far away, then…shit. Just get out of there, okay? He can move faster than you can, faster than anyone can, except for Doud and me, but he can't do it for very long. If you see him and he doesn't see you, just hide. Get out of his line of sight."

"Right. Hide. I can do that." A shiver. Fresh memory of Barstow, the monster, the wall, Doud staring up at her, roaring with hunger. Oh, fuck.

Peering in windows, he said. "I don't hear or see anyone. Maybe they aren't here."

"Yeah," she said, wrapping her arms around herself. "Maybe they went out for a bite." It was strange, and completely inappropriate, but she found his accent, the tunes and bells of his European legacy, soothing, comforting. She wished he'd keep talking.

"I'll go in, but I want to check out the backyard first." Heading around the corner of the house, a slice of shadow cast from the roof quickly slid up his body, eclipsing his head.

Leaning back against the Ferrari's driver's side door, she felt the hot metal even through her clothes. Fuck this. Bag open, Zippo and pack out. Lighting up, she inhaled a thick cloud of cool smoke. *Oh, yeah. Better than sex.*

Finishing, she flicked the cigarette away. The sun was mean, brutal. Shading her eyes, she glared up at it. Can it really be this hot? Sergio had vanished into the shade along the side of the house. She didn't want to follow, but it was better than waiting out in the heat.

Shade flowed up her side as she rounded the corner, a comforting cool. Sergio, she could see, was standing next to the rock close to the fence, near enough to identify, but too far away to see well.

Then there were two people, both too far away to see well. One was Sergio, hands on the fence, leaning forward, canting himself up on the tips of his expensive Italian boots. The other was a smoking, burning, stumbling wreck, coming around the far side of the rock. Face hidden by shadow, distorted by blackened, swollen skin, she couldn't put a name to the face or the body. Beginning with a heavy thud in her chest, her heart raced.

Vince?

Scream damnit! But she couldn't. Run damnit! But she couldn't. In the cool shade next to the house, she was frozen, trapped by her own fright.

Then she saw the clothes. She'd bought them only a day before.

Her heart beat in a different tempo. Oh my god, came her realization: It's Doud.

Planes of light cut across his face, showing cracks that oozed tears, skin split and peeled, eyes like dried eggs. He was the color of a turkey right out of the oven, skin crisped, blackened.

Too far away, and probably too hurt, he couldn't seem to see her. Sergio, though, was closer. Much closer.

Even from her distant vantage point, she saw his slumped body change: shoulders and head lifting, trying to focus beyond the damage done to his lenses, the cooked orbs.

His recognition of who was standing in front of him obvious, Doud took one step, then two, then he was rushing forward.

Oh, no. Oh, god.

One day, back when she was in college and trying to pick a subject to spend her entire life doing, she and a few friends had gone out for beer. Nothing special about it, save the time and the weather. Late November, snowstorm.

As the only one with a car, she drove. Bundled up in her best coat, buried under four thick sweaters, it was like driving in a deep sea or space suit. She could barely move but wasn't freezing, which seemed to be more important at the time.

At an intersection of two slick roads, a light had gone from yellow and for a second she'd forgotten it was November and a snowstorm. Halfway through, she'd realized two things: that it really was November and in the middle of a snowstorm and that a moving van, which had also forgotten the month and the weather, was barreling at them from the right.

Doud hazed with speed, his body moving too fast to see clearly, and crossed the space between Sergio and himself in the time it took her vision to slide from one man to the other. The air, caught between his steps, tore with dull, reverberating thunder.

At the sound, Sergio spun away from the fence. By then Doud was halfway between them. In the instant it took realization to appear on Sergio's face, Doud was there.

More thunder broke, crashed. Doud met Sergio. Both of them now moving too fast, she couldn't see what was happening. They weren't two men fighting in the desert, they were whirlwinds, twisters, cyclones of fists and hands, legs and bodies.

For Shelly, back in Providence, Rhode Island, seeing that approaching truck, and now in Needles, watching the two men: time stopped. The truck coming, the license plate readable.

Watching Sergio and Doud, or at least their blurred, accelerated forms, and, just like during that road trip, she knew that someone she cared about was going to die unless she did something, and quickly.

One step. No idea how she did it, but she had. Keep moving, keep moving. She had no idea what she'd do when she got there, if she got there, but move your damned ass. Another step. It wasn't that far, wasn't that far at all. Just a few hundred or so feet. A couple of seconds, a few more, a few less to get there. Another step, and she remembered a Massachusetts plate, VLM 069, and cranking the wheel, desperately trying to get the car away from the impact.

Almost there. Near enough to make out more of them, see that they weren't just whirlwinds, twisters, or cyclones, but two men. One slightly taller (Sergio), one slightly smaller (Doud). Clearly, Sergio punching, fist the velocity of a pistol shot. Doud, the other, stepping aside, letting the blow pass by.

Peterbilt. That was it: a Peterbilt truck heading at them, relentless and inevitable, accompanied by the thick bellow of rubber skidding on ice.

Doud was burning. Pausing their fight, an eternity for them, the flicker of an eye for her, she could see that his face was blackened from the heat of friction.

The truck, its tires, hadn't wanted to stop. It had smashed into the side of her car, breaking a window, showering them with cubed glass. Action and reaction; her car had responded, moving sideways, its tires unable to grip the icy asphalt. Later, she'd figured that without the ice, the energy of the accident would have traveled through the car and killed them all.

She was near enough now to feel her own flesh begin to crisp, the prelude to her own blisters, then her own burning. The desert, already hot, broiled, steamed from their fight. They were like dangerous, fast, massive machines, as dangerous and fatal as that truck had been, and then, as now, she was right in the path.

"Look at me, you fuckers! Look at me!" Shouting against their sonic booms: "Stop it! Stop fighting!"

The wind ebbed, the storm died down.

Stumbling exhausted, bruised, possibly even broken, Sergio fell back against the mass of the rock.

Action and reaction: Doud also stepped back. Blinking, lids skidding over dry, inflamed eyes, he finally, painfully, saw her. When it came, his voice was crisped, fried: "Shelly?"

"Yeah," she said, panting, "me. Crap." The last because she couldn't get enough air in her lungs. After a few breaths, she tried again. "I'm here, Doud. Do you see me standing here?"

He nodded.

"Good. Fuck," she coughed, adrenaline slowly leaving her still-tensed body, its departure making her shake. "Shit," she wheezed.

Doud's head swung, Sergio catching his attention again. Burned skin cracking over his knuckles, his hands curled into fists.

"Stop it, for Christ's sake!" she shrieked. "He's not going to do anything. Back the fuck off. Back off!" Legs throbbing with angry cramps, she ran between them. "Stop it. Calm down, okay? Shit! He's not going to do anything, okay? He came to help."

Coming closer, she felt a bolt of fear: was he still Doud, her friend, or had he become a monster again? That thing that'd looked up at her from a field of dead, dried weeds?

The bolt retreated, faded though. His face was a mask of pain, but didn't look desperate, or needy. Suspicion, fear, exhaustion, yes, but not hunger. Trying to speak, all that came from his mouth was a horrible squeak.

But what about Sergio? Twisting around, she saw him straighten himself up. At his sides, his fingers were also clenched tight.

She was worried about him, that he might leap back into the fight, but then those same hands went to his shirt, flicked down the front, trying to brush away dust, shoo away wrinkles.

"He—"came a squeak, and she went back to Doud. Mouth working yet only broken noises fell out. Lips swollen and weeping, his faced was blistered, swollen and puffy.

"Oh, sweetie," she said. "You look like shit."

A grin, then, cooked skin rippling, threatening to rip. Christ, don't do that she wanted to say, but caught herself. His face might have been a ruin, but his eyes still gleamed and sparked. Still ready to fight.

"Relax. Just relax. Listen to me, okay? He's here to help. You don't know what's going on. No, don't look at him, look at me." Easing towards him, she softened her tone. "He didn't go to LA to get you, he came to make sure you were okay. To warn you. I don't know what that freak told you, but he's a fucking liar. Sergio doesn't want to hurt you."

"I don't believe—" His voice was still ruined, as wrecked as his face and his body, but it was getting stronger, more distinct.

"Shut up!" she snapped. "I don't know what shit Vince has been feeding you, or what you imagined has been going on, but I know better. Sergio doesn't want to hurt you. He never did. In fact he—"

My god, he was healing. It wasn't like a film, but rather something too easily missed if not watched carefully. His skin wasn't losing years, but rather just an hour or two: swollen tissue tightening; bright red and crusty black burns fading; eyes becoming bright and glossy.

I wish I could do that. The main course, an item from column B right there in her mind. How wonderful, never to get any older, never get sick, to be totally unique. Special. Never just a part of the crowd, never just be plain, ordinary, Shelly.

She had to put it out of her mind. "Just listen, okay? Vince was the only one after you. Yeah, Sergio made him, that's true, but he never wanted to kill you. Vince left that creep for you, that monster. Vince was the one who wanted you to come here."

"That doesn't make any sense," he said, shaking his head.

"Look at me, Doud. Just look and think, for god's sake. Do you really think he's dangerous? Really? It's Sergio. You know him, knew him." That was a mistake, lots of bad blood there. Think, dummy. "I have proof that he's not the creep you think he is. Okay? Proof positive, right here in front of you."

"Go on, Shelly. Tell me," he said, losing a bit of his angry rumble. Confusion, definitely, but the fog was lifting from his vision.

"Me. Do you really think he's some kind of psycho if he would pick me up and let me tag along all the way up here? He could have killed me miles back there, drank me up and spit out my bones into the damned desert, and you'd never have been the wiser. I'm here, because he let me come along, because he wants to help!"

"She's right," Sergio said, from behind her. "About it all. Vince said he was going to go after you and I…I just didn't want you to get hurt. I wanted to warn you."

Doud's renewed sight tracking back and forth between the two of them, Sergio and Shelly, measuring, calculating.

"I know you. And I don't believe you," he said, to him, not her.

Oh, no, oh, shit, oh, no. "Fuck you, Doud. Haven't you been listening to what I've been—"

"No more questions. No more doubts." Never taking his attention from Sergio: "I'm going to kill Vince. If you want to help, then help. If not, then I'm going to kill you, too."

"I never wanted to hurt you," Sergio quickly said.

Doud didn't reply. He was too busy concentrating on the horizon. After a time, he said: "You didn't kill her. Maybe that does count for something."

Shelly piped up. "We're here for you. Just give us the word and we'll do it."

"No." Two people talking as one. Sergio and Doud glanced at her, then stared at each other.

Doud was the first to reply: "No, you're leaving. Get out of here."

"No way. No fucking away. I told you, I'm in on this. I have to see it through. I told him, I told you, hell, I told you before, back there—"

"Shelly, please," Doud's new eyes were gazing intently into her tired, middle-aged ones. "I'm not asking you this time. You don't have a choice. Too many people have died. I couldn't save any of them." After a deep breath: "That changes, right now. I couldn't save them, but I can save you. Get away from here. I don't want anything to happen to you." To Sergio: "How did you get here?"

"I drove, my car's over—" Sergio started.

"Give her the keys."

She caught the tossed key ring, glimmering metal in the sunlight. "I want to help," was all she could say.

"I know you do. Thank you. But you have to go. I'm sorry I dragged you into this." Shading his vision with the back of his hand, he peered back from where he'd come, seeing something unwelcome. "You have to go. Now."

"I don't want to go. Damnit, I'm here, you're my friend and—"

"You are my friend, my best friend, and I don't want to lose you. Get in the car." Smooth now, totally healed, his face could finally show. "He's coming. You have to go. Now. Please."

"I don't want to lose—" barely whispered. Her cheeks were wet, not blood this time.

"We have to get going. Are you ready?" This to Sergio.

The other man nodded, lips tight in certainty.

"Go, Shelly. Save yourself. For me," Doud said, grinning weakly. He signaled to Sergio and they pivoted, began walking towards the road, the open desert.

Clutching the keys too tightly, the metal biting her palm, she watched them go.

Then, after they'd faded to wavering outlines, she relaxed her hand, realizing what she held: Ferrari, Italian-engineered reality. A way out. A very fast way out.

Sergio and Doud faded into heat mirages. And she knew what she had to do.

CHAPTER 34

Tʜᴇ ᴅᴇsᴇʀᴛ ᴡᴀs ᴀɴ anvil, pounded by the relentless hammer of the sun.

That was in front of them. Behind was the rock, the house, and a cloud of dust signifying Shelly's departure. *Thank god.*

With her gone, that left only one other thing behind them: Vince.

"We have to get ready." Careful to watch the desert, not Sergio. "Do you understand?"

"Got it. I mean, yes, I understand."

Vince, who was coming, the desert, which was brutally beating down on them…all that, and still Doud's mind drifted to music. After all these years Sergio's voice still made him think of licorice-colored records spinning under the needle of a phonograph, brilliant sounds managing to come through the scratches, the pops, the grooves cut in the disc. Wonderful music.

"You're going to help, right? I need to know," Doud said, still not looking. If Sergio's speaking made him think of wonderful music, what would his face bring to mind? *Can't afford that right now.*

"Yes, I am. I want to stop him."

"You're going to have a chance to prove that soon enough," he said, risking a quick glance at Sergio. "But as far as I know, he's not the only problem. Understand?"

"I understand. I hear you."

"Good," was all Doud could say. Seeing him *had* brought more than music to mind. Too much more. Dizzying more. Confusing more.

From Sergio to behind them. The brutalized soil of the desert, but between the rock and the wall was a blur, a streak of acceleration distorting the hot air.

Risky, burning himself up like that, running so fast. He'll need to eat soon. The blur congealed as it got closer, a form emerging. Arms, legs, the knob of a head on top. In the middle of the desert, a cold chill: *that's what he's planning to do. Me. Or anyone close by.*

"We're going to kill him," he said to Sergio.

"I know that. That's what I'm here for. I should have done it before."

"Yes, you should have. This is your fault. All of this. All the people he killed are because of you." *This is your fault, and you are mine.*

"I know that, goddamnit. I know! I just couldn't deal with being alone anymore. It was okay at first, but then he started making a game of it. I hated that, tried to teach him to be more like you, never to forget the price we have to pay. I guess I mentioned you too many times. He liked that even less."

The form was growing more detailed, his shock waves and ripples fading, rolling away in surges of compressed air. *He's slowing down.* "He'll be here soon," Doud scowled, concentrating on Vince. "Ready?"

"Yes. Yes, I am." There was a pause, a rest in the melody of his voice, then: "Listen. I know he's coming, but there's something I have to say. When he said he was going to track you down, I went after him. I don't know why I did that, but damnit, I did.

I could have let him get you, but I didn't. Do you know what I'm trying to tell you?"

Face appearing out of his acceleration distortion, wind-streaked mask materializing out of a wavering desert mirage, he saw Vince was grinning from ear to ear, showing many teeth.

"No, I don't," Doud said, yelling over a thunder crack of broken air, the herald of Vince's arrival.

CHAPTER 35

"Surprise, surprise!" Vince said, tracking back and forth between them, eyes stopping at Sergio. "Now, I could be mistaken, but didn't you say you wouldn't come back?"

"I never said that," Sergio said, stepping back, away from him.

Vince's smirk grew, from wry and superior to an expression of rich pleasure. It made Doud even more furious, but he had no idea why and didn't have a lot of time to think about it.

"Well, I'm glad you came. Really, truly. Maybe when this is over we could run to town to get a bite. Or two, or three."

"Fuck you."

"Later, after dinner, or at least after I eat. I'm pretty fucking hungry." The grin didn't waver, fade, or change from who it was pointed at: Doud.

Fuck you… Doud wanted to say, echoing Sergio. Echoing Sergio? Really? The both of them, thinking the same thing, saying the same thing? That made him pause, if just for a second.

Then Vince rushed straight for him.

In that thin slice of a time between Vince *there* and Vince *gone*, Doud lit his own fire, fueled by blood and water, and quickened to match his velocity.

Vince disappeared, Doud accelerated. Vince reappeared, their speeds matching, frame of reference to frame of reference.

There was barely four feet between them, Vince still smirking, but now his brows lifted in frightened knowledge that he'd given Doud too much of a lead. He'd lost his element of surprise.

Swinging, fist breaking the sound barrier halfway, air thundering away from his knuckles, Doud aimed at his chest. Fast enough, strong enough, and that would have been it: a crushing, killing blow. *If* he was fast enough.

Wasn't. Vince danced aside. Knuckles coming faster than sound only grazed his chest, missed and in Doud's mind, again, the thought: *No!*

Inertia carried him past, giving the other man a perfect opportunity. Both arms down, a hammer blow to his back. Body continuing to follow his fist, Doud kept going, but the impact of Vince's fists was too powerful. Feet slipping, Doud awkwardly began to slide to the earth. At their speeds, the world a Teflon landscape. It took skill to stay on his feet, and even with his years of experience, Doud just couldn't.

The pain of broken bones. He had no idea how many, or how badly, but at least one of them was. The agony of the breaking remained with him as he flew forward, rushing to the ground.

Luckily, Doud had enough presence of mind to roll, to spin, so that he'd land on his back, leaving his hands free to defend himself.

Then he was on his back, sliding along the ground, his head burning, streaks of smoke tickling by his eyes, as his momentum continued to push him along.

His impetus soon deserted him, and he came to a standstill. Pain had washed away his vision, obscuring it with stars, but now that he'd stopped moving, his full vision returned. Bending his neck, he scanned around and saw Vince, a dozen feet away, darting towards him.

Come on! Get on your feet. Twisting himself around, agony returning, he crawled to his hands and knees. All the time carefully, knowing one wrong move and he'd slip and fall again.

All the time aware of Vince, he couldn't afford any more mistakes. *Come on, come on, come on*! Feet flat on the ground now, balance here, leverage there, he pushed.

Cautiously, carefully, Doud made the careful climb back up to standing. With each movement concentrating on not falling, and trying not to think about where Vince might be.

Then Doud was there, back on his feet.

Then Vince was there, with a blow aimed straight at Doud's head.

Rippling shockwaves peeled off Vince's fist as it approached him. Swiveling, pushing backwards, Doud ducked back to avoid the blow. Finding some traction but not enough, his feet began to slip again. Skittering across the gritty soil, his feet became as fast as Vince's fist, kicking up sonic booms, snaps of broken air around his ankles.

Doud stared at the approaching fist with pure detachment. Nothing flashed before his eyes, no history, no memory, no smells, no visions, no tastes, no feeling.

It was over. The monster had won.

Then a dark, wavering shape came impossibly fast from the side, interrupting the inevitability of Vince's fist. The unknown came, moving faster than either Vince or Doud, deflecting, smashing into Vince, tossing him aside and off-balance.

Unsure of what he was seeing, Doud could only stare as Vince was swept away by the dark interruption.

Vince was hurt, but exactly how much, Doud couldn't tell. Having gone too fast for too long, he felt his body cramp with exhaustion and hunger. Vince began a roll, curling himself into a ball against his own pain.

The dark form resolved itself, lowering from its dangerous speed: arms and legs, a torso and a head.

Sergio.

Watching, seeing, realizing what had happened, Doud himself slowed down, disconnecting his biological accelerator. The world became noisy, loud, and discordant, as sound caught up. Light, previously rose-colored, Doppler-shifted by their increased pace, became totally transparent.

Walking instead of running, his craving stomach doubled him over, the hunger having been awakened by his exhaustion. It was demanding food, but still on its leash.

For the time being, he was still Doud.

"Come on," Sergio said. "He's down, but not out. Let's get the hell out of here."

Reaching up, taking the offered hand, he let Sergio pull him to his feet.

CHAPTER 36

Tₕₑy didn't pick a direction, they just went. No discussion, no debate. They just moved.

The weaker of the two, Doud, saw the flat, blank slate of the open desert but also Sergio's back, his quickly pumping legs and, periodically, his face, peering behind, making sure Doud was following.

Each step was a rusty knife scraping up and down Doud's back, reminding him with too-sharp clarity of his injuries. Each tread was also a hollow reverberation, an exhausted reminder that he was more than a few pints low. But he still ran, trailing Sergio as they went off in the general direction of *away*.

Having to know, he glanced back: Vince was there, behind them, but now just a small, dark figure on his knees in the middle of the flat nothing of the desert.

As they ran farther, Vince shrank, diminished until he was nothing but a tiny black dot.

Still, they kept running, making the dot smaller and smaller, putting more and more distance between them.

Just as Doud began to figure that Vince was, hopefully, far enough away, his pains and the howling urgency of his belly came back, louder, much more demanding.

"Wait," he croaked the next time Sergio checked on him.

Sergio did, trotting to a stop. "You okay? Hanging in there?"

Nodding, Doud dropped to his knees. "Just…need—" His chest was tight, heart loud in his ears. "Rest a bit."

"Sure. No problem." Heaving gasps. "But not for long. He's going to figure out where we went and come after us."

Doud nodded again, understanding but unable to say so. For a minute, he just breathed, in and out, trying to give his body a chance to heal. Finally, after what seemed to be an eternity, he managed to croak out, "Thank you. For back there."

Sergio didn't respond at first. Instead he just looked at him, a strange expression on his features. "Well, yeah, I couldn't just let him do that to you. It didn't seem right."

"It's…I'm glad you did." He felt his strength returning. Carefully, he straightened up.

"I know I shouldn't have. But I did. I hope that counts for something."

"What do you mean?" Maybe he hadn't recovered as much as he hoped he had, was too tired to hear exactly what Sergio was saying. "I don't understand."

"Back there, LA, and Barstow, too. I couldn't let him kill you."

"I'm glad. I appreciate it. I'm sorry I doubted—"

"Just don't forget it. That's all I'm saying. After this, you go back to your life, I'll go back to mine and you'll never see me again."

"If that's what you want. But I don't think it's going to be that simple."

"Then you'd better get it over with. But I'm not going to just fucking take it," Sergio said, hands returning to fists.

"I don't understand what you're saying. I'm not going to do anything to you. You saved me. I didn't think you would, but you did. I thought you were just like him"—Doud gestured behind them—"but I can see that you're not. I need your help. I think you need mine."

Bit by bit, the fury faded from Sergio's face, the white from his knuckles. "Yes, I do."

"I thought you were like him, but I don't think that now."

"I'm not. Not at all. I used to be scared of him, but now I just hate his guts. Early on, I thought it would be good, have a life together, you know? But he didn't want that." He paused, thinking. "In the end, he was more like you than I wanted. Get what you wish for, right?"

"What do you mean? I'm sorry. I just don't understand."

"Like you. Don't lie to me. It took me a few years and a lot of thinking, but I finally figured it out. You told me, remember? Told me how this always happens, how you always…" After swallowing hard: "You killed them, didn't you? All of them. Like you tried to do with me. Anyone gets close, and that's it. The kiss of death. I figured that since you did it so much you must like it."

Doud got his lips and mouth to work. "No…" was all that came out.

"How fucking stupid is that? Running from one to another. But I tried to save you. I just hope you'll remember that. Just let me walk away."

"No, that's not it. You don't understand."

"I loved you, I thought you loved me. Then you tried to kill me. Make me understand, Doud. Explain it to me. Come on, you owe me that much," Sergio said.

Mind swinging off-balance, dazed, Doud wanted to put out a hand, grab hold of anything concrete, restore his equilibrium, but they were standing in the middle of the desert. Just the two of them. Sergio. Doud.

Abruptly he wanted to explain, to tell him that he was wrong, that he didn't enjoy those deaths, that he did it out of necessity, to keep monsters like Vince away, that he hadn't done it to keep them away when they'd gotten too close—

No sounds, no speech. Mouth open, nothing emerged. As if standing in front of a mirror, he saw his own features reflected back. It was too easy to see it Sergio's way, see what he'd become.

Sergio's gaze, however, had drifted back to the distance, past Doud's shoulder. "You might want to hurry."

Following Sergio's finger, he saw the house and the stone were miniatures in the great distance. The rock, a pebble on the flat horizon, the house barely visible next to it. But between the rock and the house was a new element to the scene, a dust cloud, evidence of something fast approaching.

Both of us. It's catching up to both of us.

"Doud," Sergio said, again a tune from an Old World music box, "tell me what happened. Why it happened. I need to know."

"I believed you were…like the others," he said. *No, all wrong. That's not it. I'm not saying it right.* "I thought you were killing but not caring; that what I'd given you was nothing but a new way to hurt people. That's why I did it. I couldn't live with creating anyone like that, having that on my conscience."

"That's what you thought? That I was going to kill for kicks? Shit."

"That's why. I don't like it. I never have. I've never found anyone who understood what I was offering. I imagined you were like those others, that I had to stop you."

"You could have asked. Explained it to me. I remember you said that it was important that I be with you, and not just want to…eat to live, all of that. I heard you, but I hoped you'd talk to me first, not just try to kiss my life away. That's when I figured it out. That you liked it, I mean. Or I figured you did. I don't know what's going on." Facing the approaching whirlwind of dust: "You should have talked to me. I would have listened. Why didn't you, Doud? Why the hell didn't you?"

Not having an answer, he had nothing to say. *He's coming closer*, was all that came to mind though, as he stole a look behind them.

"Didn't I mean anything to you? I hoped I did. You meant something to me. Hell, I came looking for you after all this time. I've missed you."

Why didn't I talk to him? He wasn't like them. He wasn't. Say it, say what you've wanted to say. "I-I missed you, too."

The churning dust, and the thing inside it, was imminent. *Run.* He wanted to sprint, to burn the liquid life remaining in his belly in one frantic *get away.*

Get away. From guilt, from shame. But he couldn't. He wouldn't. He had to face it. All of it.

What if he'd held Sergio's hand, listened, talked, explained, worked it out? Sergio would never have become a thing, a monster. Agony, but not from hunger.

Heartache.

Looking out towards to the advancing dust devil so he didn't have to see Sergio's face, he tried to be calm. When he felt he could speak again without catch or quaver, he did. "I'm sorry. I should have talked to you. Explained it all. Worked it out. I was frightened, and not because I was scared you'd become that"—a tilt of his head to the whirlwind—"but because you'd have gotten too close to me. Forgive me. Please."

It was the most important thing he'd ever done: *Forgive me.* A plea had been there, in those portraits painted in blood and fluid, but he'd never come close to honestly capturing it before. The subjects had been there, their faces and their essences, captured and preserved, but he'd never said what honestly needed to be said.

Forgive me.

Understanding. Hard, painful, and direct. It had never been about art. Why paint? Why hang them on walls? Why give them to people like Shelly to display for everyone to see?

All because he hadn't been able to ask, not once in all those years. So he'd displayed himself, looped picture wire around his neck, and hung himself on gallery walls. Art not for absolution. Art perpetually, eternally about guilt.

They were dead, those faces done in blood. But there was one, just one, the only face in his whole life that meant anything except nutrition, or a reprieve from loneliness.

Desire, want, need. What he wanted to say stayed trapped in his mind, unsaid. One hundred and fifty years of inertia keeping his mouth shut. Habits dying hard, long habits close to undying.

"I dreamed of you. I didn't really want to, but I did. I'd lie awake at night, think: *what's he doing now? Does he think about me? What does he think about me?* Then I'd hate myself for being so stupid, carrying a torch for a man who wanted to kill me. But I did," Sergio said.

Stinging in Doud's eyes, and not just from grit borne by the steady desert breeze. "I—" he began.

"Quiet. Let me finish. I'd think of you. I didn't want to, but I did. I'd either miss you or I'd figure out that you were just someone else who'd hurt me."

"I never realized, not once, that I had it all wrong, that you really were that guy I sat under elephants with, who said we had all the time in the world together." Snorting to himself Sergio ran fingers through his hair. "It's weird, to be surprised. You probably get that too, right? Too many years, lots of fancy new machines, always the same kind of people doing the same things over and over again. I like it, being surprised, I mean. It's new, it's different, and that's rare." Quickly shutting his eyes, not wanting to, not quite ready to see what was getting nearer, he continued:. "You're damned rare, too. What we had. I forgive you, Doud. I forgive you."

Say it. Say what you've wanted to say for all those years. Just three little words. Say it.

"Get ready." Doud said instead, urgently, voice crackling with more than a just little fear. "He's here."

He's too powerful. We're not. He doesn't care about anything. We care too much. "Sergio—" The other man spun and even though Doud could tell his body was bunched with expectation, ready for battle, he was smiling. Not Vince's wry, superior smirk, but an expression of…? Hot, dry desert air, grit and sand blowing everywhere, kicked up by the coming monster, but Doud's sight burned and watered for a different reason. Sergio's smile was the greatest image, the most wonderful sight Doud had ever seen. An ache, then, to hold it, capture it, to paint him, but not to appease, or hang himself on a gallery wall. Brush to canvas, instead, to be able see that face, that wonderful expression, forever.

"Yes?"

"N-nothing. I was just going to say—we'll win. Don't worry."

"Well, that makes one of us. But thanks for the vote of confidence."

The sun flickered, glazed over by dirt and dust kicked up by the wind billowing into their faces, hiding the beast. Noise came through though, a deep roar, even through the obscuring dust.

Come on, Doud thought, taking deep breaths, preparing his body, readying his mind: *Come on.*

Then it was there, in a spray of gravel, a squeal of tires on hard yellow earth. A red, fast, high-octane engine, and a blast of strident sound. A hand slapping the horn.

"Shelly?" Doud murmured.

"The one and only. I've been back and forth across this damned place for an hour trying to find you two." Getting out from behind the wheel, she drew an arm across her brow, wiping away dust and sweat. "I think I fucked up your transmission," this to Sergio. "Been a while since I've driven a stick."

"What are you doing here?" the car's owner snapped back, eyes wide and unbelieving.

Absurdity, relief, exhaustion...*laugh!* But no guffaw, or even just a low giggle. One hundred and fifty years and, Doud remaining Doud, he just couldn't do it. In the air, though, along with the grit and powdered desert, were all kinds of transitions, various changes. Many smiles.

"Cavalry," she explained, reflecting Doud's expression, though not for long. "By the way, we don't have much time." Jerking her head in the general direction of behind her, she went on: "He's right behind me. Twenty minutes, but probably a helluva lot sooner, before he catches up."

CHAPTER 37

THEY LOOKED LIKE SHIT.
Sergio's clothes were torn and wrinkled, faded with grime. His face was drawn, haunted, but his dark eyes still gleamed.

Doud, though, was an outright wreck. Flashback to how he looked after the monster, the message left behind in Barstow: not that hollow or used up, but empty enough, his bones made white-ridged relief against the back of his hands, his skull shown through the thin skin of his face.

But his eyes, too, shone from their sunken depths. Light from the bottom of a well. A good light, a happy light.

"You should have been miles away," Sergio said. "What the hell are you doing here?

"Screw that. I couldn't just leave you two behind. No way, not happening. I said I was going to help and that's what I'm going to do."

"Shelly. You have to go. You can't stay here. Please."

"Doud's right. You have to get out of here. Like you said, Vince is going to be here soon. You don't want to be here when he shows up. Believe me."

"I know all that. I've seen the guy, okay? Not like you guys have, but I get the damned idea. I told you, though; I couldn't just let you two deal with this asshole on your own. All for one, right?"

"This isn't a fucking game!" Sergio snapped, harsh words popping in her ears. "He's going to be here in just a few minutes, you stupid—" Breathy pause, then: "He's hungry. Hungry, you understand? You know what I mean. Starving. Doud and I, we might be able to make it. Fight him off. I doubt it, though. But you…he's going to kill you. Maybe he'll just snap your damned neck, or suck you dry. But he's going to kill you. That's a guarantee. You have to get away from here."

"I know that, damnit. I really do. I'm not stupid, you know. But that's what you think I am, don't you? You pricks. You drag me along, shove me around, protect me, use me, but neither of you really gives a fuck about me, about what I want. Well, guess what? You can't make me leave. I'm here and I'm going to help."

"Shelly." Doud again, but this time her name, said by him, in that tone, made her look, quieted her just a little. Seeing his expression, she couldn't say anything else. "I didn't mean to get you involved. I dragged you along without thinking what you might want. You're right, I should have let you decide for yourself. I should have trusted you. I'm sorry."

Tears. *Damnit.* Face feeling sunburned with their coming, she turned around, concentrating instead on the grime fanned across the Ferrari's fender.

"I really am," Doud continued, "but you have to face reality. If you stay, you will die. I wish you could help but you can't. It's as simple as that."

"He's right," Sergio said, from nearby. Moving closer to the car, his shadow mixed with hers. "This isn't the time or place for what any of us really wants. This is survival, that's it. If you stay, Vince is going to kill you. We'll try and stop him of course, and maybe we will, but he'll probably kill one of us, as we're trying to save you. Is that what you want?"

Raising her head, she stared at him. There was anger, sure, frustration and fear, but also an unknown quantity, an element added to the Sergio she'd driven with.

She looked at Doud, but he wasn't looking at her. His eyes were only on Sergio. *That's it, right there. That's what I want.* Back and forth, Doud to Sergio, Sergio to Doud. The two of them. *That's it.*

"You two keep thinking this is the dumb bitch you've been dragging all over the place. What do I have to do to get through to you that I know what's going on here? Did I freak out when I saw you with that monster in Barstow? Did I? No, I didn't. Even when you tried to pull that fucking boogeyman act on me, scare me off, did I go running home? You, lover-boy," to Sergio, making him jerk his head at the nickname. Annoyance at first, but then the pleasant lines in his face were back. "Sure I thought you were the big, bad Sergio that Doud told me about, but I didn't stay freaked, did I? It may have taken a minute or two, but I finally figured out that you were one of the good guys. So you think you could treat me like a fucking adult?"

She glared at one, then the other, meeting their stares, but more importantly the change between them. *All the time in the world. Decades sliding by, years like minutes. Time to see everything, do everything. Knowing you're rare, special, unique. Not just a damned face, but alive. Really alive.* "So, you going to let me have my say or not?"

"We don't have any time for this—"

"Wait. Please." Doud to Sergio, then to her: "Tell us what you want. You are right. You deserve it. Just make it fast."

"Okay." *What I want.* "I've been thinking and I think I've got it figured out. See…see there's just the two of you, okay? You might be able to win, but not likely. No insult guys, but you couldn't tie your own shoelaces, let alone kick that prick's ass right now. Doud, you're five quarts low, right? Bottom of the barrel, running on empty. Fumes. You need to eat…drink, whatever the hell you do, and you need to do it soon. You also need help, someone to give you a hand. Like three against one. Got me?"

Sergio began to say something, Doud's glistening orbs got wide, but she kept going: "Take me, drink me, eat me. Put some fucking flesh on your bones. But also make me one of you. I want that." There, out in the open. Simple, straight, direct, honest: *what she wanted*. What she'd always wanted.

Doud spoke first. "No." Loud, firm. "No," repeated, even harder. "You don't know what you're saying."

"I know what I'm saying. You still think I'm dumb, don't you, Doud? Well, here's a shock and a surprise: I'm not. I've added it up. I told you, it makes sense. It makes perfect sense. I'm not thinking with anything but my brain, believe me. You need help, you need to eat and don't tell me otherwise. I know you can make others like you two. Vince is right behind me, steaming and smoking and pissed as hell. Wouldn't you rather make it three against one, rather than two against one? Tell me this doesn't make sense. Come on, I dare you."

"I won't do it. You don't know what it's like. Haven't you been listening? Haven't you?" Looking away from her, out to the empty desert, then back. "Can you kill, Shelly? You'll have to, every few months. If you don't, if you try and fight it, you'll kill anyway. You just won't be able to choose who. It'll be people you know, people you like. You'll wake with dust at your feet, guilt that never goes away."

"I know that. I understand, but it's the only way," she began. *I want this. More than anything I want this. The three of us. The only three in the whole world. Special, unique. All the time in the world.*

"You don't know. You can't know. I do. He does." A nod to Sergio, who stood there, mute, with a strange expression on his face. "You're a good friend. I care about you. You know that. I want you to be happy, to have a good life. This isn't it. What we are…it isn't good. It isn't. I know that now for sure."

"It's not about good or bad. Like you said, it's about facing facts. He's coming and you can't tell me that you and tall, dark, and handsome here, can take him out. But three of us, that's better odds. You want to know what I want, Doud? I want my friend—my friends—to be okay. I don't think that's going to happen if there's just the two of you."

It was what she wanted. But it wasn't the only thing she wanted. Years. All the time in the world. With Doud, her friend. The one person who'd cared for her. The only person she'd really cared for.

"He's right. We're not going to change you, so you might as well leave," Tall, Dark and Handsome unexpectedly said. "Go away. Do something with your life. Meet Mr. Wonderful. Live. Those are *your* facts. Get out and live."

"No, not without you guys. No way. I'm going to sit here," she said, back against the hot metal car door "and wait until either that creep shows up, or you two come to your senses."

"Stubborn, isn't she? I can see why you two hung out together."

"She has other good qualities. Believe it or not," Doud said, sharing the same tight grin.

"You fuckers," she said, trying to laugh, wanting to join them. "Come on, think it over. Don't run away. You're always running away. This whole thing started with you freaking out and hitting the road. Well, you can't run any more. You've got to deal with this, right now, here, and you can't do it alone. We're here to help. I'm here to help. Stop being so damned frightened. Take what I'm offering and let's kick his fucking ass."

It was a long, difficult moment. Too far? Not far enough? How much do you push? Was it right to push? Conflicting thoughts buzzed in her mind, angry bees between her ears: Had she really hurt him, or just told him the truth? Was it the truth or just a selfish trick to con him into giving her what she wanted?

Sergio then walked past her, up to him, putting a hand on Doud's shoulder. It was an uncomplicated contact, transmitting basic, good, things between them.

"You're right, Shelly. You are. But I *am* going to run away. No, don't say anything. I know what I'm doing." To Sergio, still close by: "Will you come with me?"

It took the other man a second to reply, but when he did he was strong and sure. "Absolutely."

Before she could say anything else, Doud walked up to her. "Shelly," he said, looking hard at her. "Thank you. For everything. You've been a good friend, my best friend, but you are not going with us. Don't say anything. Let me finish."

His rough, burned hand reached out, took hers. "I know it's not what you want, and it may not make sense, but it's what has to happen. We might not make it, but Vince is not going to win. I promise that. I think I have it figured out."

"Well, I'm glad you do but—"

"I've made mistakes. Too many. I used to do what I hoped was the right thing, to make it all better, but I was lying to myself. Like you said, it's time to face facts." A glance at Sergio, then back to her: "I know the truth now. If I do what you want, we may beat him, but it would be a mistake, another damned mistake, but this time it would be you. I have to make this right, and I can't do that by changing someone I care about into another monster, even if it'll save my life, and someone I care about."

Sergio beamed with affection. "You want to help? Get in the car and drive away. Have a good life, Shelly. You deserve it." Opening the car door: "Maybe we'll go to a movie again."

Nothing to say. Instead, tears. It was over, all done. *What I want* and *what I* really *want* gone. Dreams evaporating. But that wasn't what made her cry, painted her face with salty drops, smears of cool moisture.

Doud, her friend...*gone*.

The interior of the car was hot. Too hot, but she didn't complain. She awakened the Italian horses. Door still ajar, she lifted eyes to Doud, finally finding her voice. "Good luck," was all she said. Of all the words she'd ever spoken, the millions, the thousands, those two were the only ones that mattered.

Smiling weakly, he reached into the hot interior and put a hand on her shoulder. So few words spoken, a handful in so many years, silence saying all he needed to say.

With the shutting of the finely crafted door, she was on the inside, he on the outside. Moving back, he waved, the gesture obviously making him uncomfortable but done nonetheless.

Sergio joined him, both of them fitting together smoothly. Then they turned, moved away. Normally at first, then faster and faster, until the dust of their acceleration hazed, then totally obscured them.

Aiming the car in no particular direction, she began to drive. Engine too loud, fine engineering operating at full throttle, she couldn't hear herself think, which was exactly what she wanted.

CHAPTER 38

Ow long had they been running? Miles? Hours? Minutes? He hadn't been keeping track, at least not in those measurements.

When he did think, feel, and hope that they'd run far enough, Doud held his arm out in front of Sergio, who heeded the gesture. They eased, then stopped.

It wasn't the only unspoken communication between them since they'd started running. When he glanced over his shoulder at Sergio, he found the other man staring back. Sprinting across the flat, hot wasteland in their tandem, syncopated strides, he would *know* and turn to see Sergio grinning back at him. He, always, would beam back. It was like nothing had happened, no time had passed between them.

Then he made his decision. Stopping, their silent unity remained. Panting, they smiled at each other, neither able to catch and hold enough dry air to speak.

Doud looked up. The desert. All around them. Nothing human, nothing civilized. Just hard-baked desert.

I hope this'll do. It has to. It has to.

The sun was just beginning its descent towards dusk, hanging bright, red, and heavy in an ending quarter of the sky. Not yet a sunset, still many hours of light left, but the colors were just beginning to emerge. Cinnabar, iodine, sangria, ruby, dandelion, amber, a preliminary swash of soft colors, preamble to a final, beautiful execution.

From the sunset to Sergio, and Doud dreamed of painting again. True, honest, painting. The way Sergio stood, wheezing, chest rising and falling as he drew in air, blew out whatever his body didn't need. The shape of his skull, the plane of his cheeks, the rise and gentle irregularities of his nose. Lips, yes, but also the elegance of his neck, the architecture of his ears. Eyes, absolutely, and looking into them Doud could think of nothing but painting, the sunset, the desert, Sergio, but most of all his lovely eyes.

It was good. Oh, it was so good. He wished as hard as he could that somehow he could bring up his hand, hold a brush, have a surface, any surface, to capture him. It was so wonderful, not to feel a tug of guilt anymore. All that was gone, absolved. Seeing himself for the first time, really seeing, he understood the illusions he'd drawn around himself, seen his true colors.

The sun was inching down the sky. Aqua, cinnamon, bronze, rose, a licking flame. Doud wanted to paint it, too. To hold forever the coming sunset of a world that was really much richer, more colorful, subtle, and beautiful that he had realized.

"Tired?" Sergio asked, rubbing the back of his neck. "I am."

With a nod, Doud straightened, feeling his body pop, crackle and groan in complaint. But the physical pain was to his hunger pangs. Glancing at the back of his hands, he saw bones, white and raised like ridges of dirty ivory, tendons like shallow cables buried under thin, brittle skin. Flesh retreating from his fingernails like claws. Hungry hands. Starving hands.

The pain agreed, surging agony up his chest, making his mouth yawn, gasping for anything liquid, or living. Covering his mouth with the back of one of his desiccated hands, he laughed. "That was a yes."

"Hungry, too," Sergio said, noticing what Doud had tried to hide. "Same here."

"Shouldn't be too much longer." Behind them, back the way they'd come, there was a rippling mirage heading towards them.

"I've figured it out."

Doud looked at him, trying to see him without a painter's concentration, but with better, more realistic vision, searching for suspicion in his expression, fear on his face. Perhaps too much of his romantic, artistic view remained behind, clouding what he saw, but he swore he didn't see anything like suspicion, nothing even close to fear.

Sergio flashed him another smile, and that's all that Doud could see: Sergio, happy. Despite it all, the past and what was going to happen—what Doud hoped would happen—he smiled back at him. "I'm sorry," he said, joy quickly fading, losing out against the weight of reality.

With a wave of his hand, Sergio dismissed Doud's regret. "Don't be. You're right. It's the only thing that makes sense. I just hope your plan works."

So do I. "We don't have much time." The mirage was a man, tearing through the hot desert atmosphere. "I wish we had more."

"So do I. But, you know, even after all of this, all the shit and stupid mistakes, it still feels like I went out for a drink and a smoke. A few minutes, you know, rather than all those years."

"I feel the same way." His sight had begun to burn, vision waver. If he said anything, he'd start to cry. *Not good, need the moisture.* To hide it, he glared at the figure defining itself, mirage becoming cohesion, form becoming recognizable.

"Here he comes."

Traveling fast, tearing across the flat plain at them, unmistakable: *Vince.*

Clenching his fists, Doud fought to keep from jumping to speed. *Reflex.* Belly empty, run dry, he was only a few seconds away from surrendering to the hunger. *Control. Stay in control.*

"You're in no shape. Let me get his attention."

Then, with a booming rush, a harsh wind, Sergio was gone, air whirling to fill in his place. Dust and grit stung Doud's eyes. So that's what it looks like, he thought, fascinated. A few dozen feet in front of him, a median point between the approaching Vince and where Sergio had been standing, a tremendous storm blasted into existence.

A hurricane, a typhoon in the middle of the desert, in the still blasting heat of a fading day. But it was a quick turmoil, a sudden and angry dance of air, the fight between Vince and Sergio, as seen by Doud.

There one instant, then not. The storm was gone, its only legacy the sound of sand and stones falling back to earth. Two men where the typhoon had been. Sergio holding his side and panting with exhaustion. His face was drawn and callow, shrunken from burning so much liquid fuel in the fight, the speed at which he'd had to move.

It hurt, to see him like that. Doud wanted, more than anything, to burst into speed himself, and go to him. To hold him, make it all okay.

Then he looked at Vince.

He, too, had changed. Sergio was shrunken, used up, but Vince was only a hint, barely a suggestion of the man he'd been before: face cavernous, skin crisped to black and seeping, bleeding red where it had split; muscles from knotted ropes to barely humming strings. Mouth…a pit, a yawning, gasping hole ringed with irregularly spaced teeth, showing a quivering, undulating throat of pink, wet tissue.

"Here!" Doud yelled, as loud as he could. "Here, here! Look here!" Waving his arms, he tried to catch the monster's attention.

The mouth squirmed with peristaltic motion, seeking moisture with ancient senses, searching for the living to drink. The eyes, pulled deep within the skull, seemed to hunt out the source. Primal, like sniffing the air with vision.

"I'm right here. Can't you see me?"

"Doud." Lips moving, throat contracting, the mouth swallowed nothing but enough desert air to be able to say his name. Finished talking, it ponderously closed, shrinking, dilating till lips met lips.

Hunger doesn't speak, doesn't know names. Minds do that. Consciousness does that. There was still a chance. Allowing himself a weak, satisfied grin, Doud kept doing his self-calming exercises, not allowing himself too much hope, or too much fear.

Sergio joined him, standing close by. It made him feel better, having him there. "That's right," he said, glaring at Vince. "Doud. You remember me, don't you? The one that Sergio talked about all the time?"

"Oh, yeah," Vince said. "I remember. Oh, yeah—" he scowled, face moving to match the emotion, the hunger shoved back down. "I'm going to kill you." To Sergio: "Then you."

"No, you're not," Doud said.

The sneer remained, but tighter, narrower. "The hell you say. The *fuck* you say."

"I *do* say. Because I know something you don't. Look behind you."

"Fuck you."

"Then I'll tell you. There's nothing behind you. Nothing but the desert."

"Trying to trick me—" Yawning, his mouth expanded again.

"Shut up, Vince." Doud was calm. His heart was beating regularly. His breathing was simple, not hissing or panicked. No anger, no fighting, no running. All he had to do was keep talking. "Be quiet and listen. There's nothing behind you but desert. Miles and miles of it. We're in front of you. We're hungry, but not as hungry as you are. You didn't think this through. The world was always there for you to feed on, but not out here."

"Fuck you, Doud. Fuck you."

Legs shifting, posture taut, Doud recognized that Vince was getting ready to accelerate. He couldn't let him.

"You can't beat both of us, Vince. You get me, Sergio gets you. You get Sergio, but I'll kill you. You're not fast enough to beat us both. And you have to beat us both, because you're too far away, Vince. There's no way you can make it back to town without feeding on us. You're not good enough. I might be able to do it, and Sergio can definitely do it, but you're too weak. I told Sergio you were stupid to come out here."

"He's right," Sergio said. "He's absolutely right. There's no way you're going to take us out, and there's no way you can make it back to town without us. You're fucked, Vince. You're majorly fucked. Doud could make it. You, though, you're a fucking asshole. A stupid fucking asshole."

Risking a glance, Doud saw Sergio's body was tight, pulled from every corner. Also ready to run, if need be.

"If you were me, then you could run back to town. Feed and return. But you're not, are you, Vince?" Doud said.

Hate me. I'm the one, the original. Sergio talked about me. Doud, Doud, Doud, Doud, Doud. I was the first, I always knew what to do. I was the original, the best. You're just a copy, sloppy seconds.

"Fuck you," Vince growled, head tilted down, teeth tight, jaw clenched. "Fuck you both," he added, slit of vision towards Sergio, jaw even more tightly clenched. "I'll see you assholes later."

Giving them his back, he was in motion. A step at first, then another, then a noble walk. *A cool walk, a man's walk*, Doud continued to think, watching him. *A man who always needs to prove he's a man.* Soon he was striding faster, then faster still. *Run, come on, run!* A slap of air, a tiny thunderclap of atmosphere forced out of the way by the blinding acceleration of a large object moving through it, and he was gone. All that was left behind was a swirling cloud of grit and gravel, dust and dirt kicked up from the desert floor, sucked along behind him.

Neither one of them said anything. In reverse of a few minutes ago, Vince shot off towards the horizon, small human figure reducing second by second, until vanishing into a distortion of speed and distance.

An indulgence, a little treat for himself, Doud let his face show relaxed pleasure, satisfaction, and accomplishment. *It worked. It really worked.*

A life of avoiding what he was, an eternity evading what he'd done, decades retreating into himself, more than a century of trying to escape. Then, in two days, trapped by a dozen or so hours, he'd had to face it all. No way out, nowhere to run.

Cracking mirrors, shattering walls, crumbling illusions. The agony of truth, the pain of knowing what he was, what he'd been doing, what had really been going on.

One hundred and fifty years, and in those few hours, those quick days, he found what he'd really been hunting for, knew what he should have done all along.

Paintings, and so evading his guilt, his responsibility. *Final, goodbye kisses* for anyone who came close: retreating from happiness, safe in his suffering.

If only it had come sooner, leaving him a few more hours, a few more minutes, a few more seconds to enjoy it.

At least he wasn't alone in that, he thought, looking to the vacant horizon and the vanishing Vince.

Doud, who'd spent a lifetime running away, finally finding what he'd always wanted, where there was nowhere left to run.

Vince, tricked into running to a place he'd never reach. They were too far out, with no one between here and town to feed on.

He was running to his death.

"It's over," Sergio said with a sigh. "We've won. Thank god," he added, focused on the distance, still watching, long after Vince was too far gone to see.

"Yes," was all Doud could say in response. The world was suddenly so much bigger. The stage they'd been performing on expanded out to the edges of the sky. Just the two of them in the middle of the desert.

No more Vince.

"What… What if he *does* make it back?"

I want to look at him forever. He's so beautiful. "He can't," Doud said, then he repeated it not so much to convince himself, but to make sure Sergio understood.

"Because you can't either, can you?" Sergio said, face frozen between emotions. "You're right, I guess. It's better this way. I'm just glad we're together."

Again, Doud's hand itched for a brush to capture him, freeze him for all time just like he was right then. Eyes, dark and lovely. The planes of his face, like a perfect execution in flawless marble.

That's what I've been missing: the only man who meant something to me, the only man I've ever wanted to be with.

Reaching out, he took Sergio's hand. "So am I."

"Hours?" Sergio said, reaching up to stroke Doud's paper dry cheek. Quivering with moisture, Doud's pupils danced in response. "Probably. Not many. Me less than you, of course. I promised you eternity. I'm sorry."

"Don't be. Years, even lots and lots of them, don't really matter, not really. Just the next few hours do," Doud said, holding his hand.

"Thank you."

"You're welcome."

"We could share, you know."

Doud, head tilted in puzzlement. "Share?"

"You know, from me to you. Give you some of what I have. It's not much, but it could buy you more time." Softly: "I don't want you to…go first. Silly, I know."

"No, it's not. You're right, we should have more time together. Forever or just a few hours, we'll enjoy what we have." Waving at the farthest edge of the perfectly level horizon, he added, "Show me your desert."

"I'd like that. I'd like that very much."

"But first," Doud said, "kiss me."

EPILOGUE

*T*HAT'S GOOD. SLOW DRAG in, then out through her nose: plume of silver smoke quickly twisted, then completely scattered by intermittent gusts of brittle desert air. *Oh, man, that's good.*

That the sun was descending, fattening, night coming, wasn't on her mind. Even the cigarette between her fingers was just a thing. A good thing, the quenching of a craving, but still just an object.

Examining the gently glowing end, she debated flicking it away, discarding the bad habit. But she didn't. *Later—well, maybe.* For now, bad or not, the cigarette felt great.

As she smoked, the sun fell farther. *Pretty. Lovely.* Taking another long drag, she puffed it out, noticing with a wry grin that it was nowhere near a ring.

A few hours before, she would have been disappointed in what had happened. How it had turned out. But smoking her cigarette and admiring the sunrise, she didn't feel that way any longer. Not at all. She hadn't really understood. Now, now she did. The smoke was nice, close to *damned* good, but the glow rising inside herself, a counterbalance to the coming night, was wonderful.

Then she saw the haze, the distortion in the air.

Fear made the desert chilly, cold. Even beginning to burn between her fingers, the cigarette was forgotten.

No, it can't be. It can't.

The form took on a shape, clarity growing by the second. A dark figure, rushing at her across the desert. Moving fast. Moving very fast.

Snapping her fingers, she sent the cigarette tumbling away, red tip a spiral in the air. *No way. I'm not going to let you.*

Instantly, she knew who it was.

A few hours before she would have felt differently. Now, though, that she knew what she really wanted in life she didn't feel fear, terror, but rather pure, hot rage.

Come on you fucking bastard. Come on! No idea, not a single one, of what she was going to do. But she was going to fight, because for the first time she had something worth fighting for. *I'm going to kick your fucking teeth down your throat*!

She'd guessed Doud's plan, worked it out while driving across the desert. It made sense. It had been a good plan, even if it meant stranding her friend, her *two* friends, out in the desert with no way of getting back. So why hadn't it worked?

Get in the car, get the hell away from there. Put a dozen, a hundred, a thousand damned miles between us. Live to fight another day. Important that: "live." Probably the most important word there ever was.

Smoke, but not hers. Straining to catch every detail, she saw the gray begin, the streamers trailing away from the figure. As he got closer, there was more and more of it. A comet, a rocket, he roared across the plain towards her, trail of kicked-up dust and thick, once gray now black, haze following behind him.

Black smoke, thin but now thick. Searing, he ran across the desert. Aflame, he grew in her vision. Burning as he sprinted, she knew Doud's plan *had* worked.

Scorching, blazing, and then he was crumbling, cinders flaring behind him. She didn't want to look, but it happened so quickly she didn't have time to turn away.

Flame to soot, soot to ash, ashes to ashes, dust to dust, then nothing but a twister of grit, a gust of hot air as he burned up. Whatever was left twirled through the air, blowing completely away. Not enough even to bury, even if she'd wanted to.

It was over. Vince was gone.

Swinging open the car door, she stopped, didn't get in. Not yet. Turning around, she threw a glance over her shoulder, out toward the flat, dry expanse.

Thanks. Probably ashes and dust as well by then, more than likely blowing in the wind, mixing with Sergio's ashes and dust. They were together. Dead, but together. Even though his absence was a serious ache in her belly, her mind, she kept her grin.

She'd found what she'd wanted all along. Now it was time to go. Getting in Sergio's car, closing the door, she cranked on the engine. Time to go back to the city, and *Objects D*, but not back to her old life.

It took being with Doud for her to finally figure it out. At first she'd gotten it all wrong, thinking what she'd wanted was what he had: immortality, being one of a kind, a rare and special being.

But that wasn't it.

It took seeing the two of them together. Sergio and Doud. Two people who were even more rare and special. Two people who cared for each other with all of their hearts.

She might not have hundreds of years, but she still had a whole world and a good hunk of time. Giving the car a drink of high octane with a push of her foot, she drove away, back to the main road, back home.

To begin her search.

ABOUT THE AUTHOR

EXTENSIVELY PUBLISHED IN SCIENCE fiction, fantasy, horror, thrillers, and nonfiction, it is in erotica that M.Christian has become an acknowledged master, with their stories repeatedly appearing in anthologies such as *Best American Erotica*, *Best Gay Erotica*, *Best Lesbian Erotica*, *Best Bisexual Erotica*, *Best Fetish Erotica*, the Mammoth Books of Erotica, and too many anthologies, magazines, and sites to name.

M.Christian's short fiction has been collected in many bestselling books in a wide variety of genres, including the Lambda Award finalist *Dirty Words* and other queer collections like *Filthy Boys* and *BodyWork* as well as erotic science fiction with *Rude Mechanicals*, *Technorotica*, *Better Than the Real Thing*, *Bachelor Machine*, *Skin Effect*, and *Hard Drive: The Best Sci-Fi Erotica of M.Christian*.

As a novelist, M.Christian has shown their monumental versatility with books such as the queer vamp novels *Running Dry* and *The Very Bloody Marys*; the erotic romance *Brushes*; the science fiction erotic novel *Painted Doll*; and the controversial gay horror/thrillers *Finger's Breadth* and *Me2*.

M.Christian is also a featured writer and managing editor for *Future of Sex* (www.futureofsex.net): "providing insights into the fascinating topic of the future of human sex and sexuality."

In addition to writing, M.Christian is a respected sex and BDSM educator, having taught classes on everything from polyamory to tit torture for venues such as the SF Citadel, Good Vibrations, COPE (in Columbus, Ohio), Beat Me In St. Louis, Winter Fire, Floating World, Sin In The City (Las Vegas), Dark Odyssey, and many others.

Visit www.mchristian.com for further information.

ABOUT QUEEN OF SWORDS PRESS

Q[UEEN OF SWORDS]{} IS an independent small press, specializing in swashbuckling tales of derring-do, bold new adventures in time and space, mysterious stories of the occult and arcane and fantastical tales of people and lands far and near. Visit us online at www.queenofswordspress.com and sign up for our mailing list to get notified about upcoming releases and offers. Or follow us on social media (@qospress on Bluesky and Instagram) so you don't miss any press news.

If you have a moment, the author would appreciate you taking the time to leave a review for this book at Goodreads, your blog or on the site you purchased it from.

Thank you for your assistance and your support of our authors.

9 798999 186681